Can God *Love* ME?

Can God *L*ove ME?

A Reassuring Testimony of God's Abounding Love

Nancy L. Anderson

Eagles Rest
Celebration, Florida

Scripture quotations noted NIV are from the HOLY BIBLE: NEW INTERNATIONAL VERSION © 1973, 1978, 1984 International Bible Society. Used by permission of Zondervan Publishing House. All rights reserved.

Scripture quotations noted KJV are from the KING JAMES VERSION

Can God Love Me?
© 2001 by Nancy L. Anderson

ISBN: 0-9705838-0-X

First printing, January, 2001
04 03 02 01   5 4 3 2 1

Book Production and Cover Design by
The 'Write' Perspective™
— *WritePerspective.com* —
Cover Illustration by Kristi Plank

Published by Eagles Rest
PO Box 470544
Celebration, Florida 34747-0544
— *www.e-eaglesrest.com* —

All rights reserved. No part of this book may be reproduced or transmitted in any form or by any means without the written permission of the author, except for the inclusion of brief quotations in a review. Printed in the United States of America.

~ DEDICATION ~

. . .those who hope in the Lord will renew their strength. They will soar on wings like eagles. . . (Isaiah 40:31)

To my husband, Carl, who has been a support and a motivator, as well as keeping me focused on this endeavor. To my eldest daughter, Julie, who God has blessed with music in her heart and with a deep desire to know and serve Him. To my daughter, Sharon, who God has blessed with the heart of a leader and with a special love for Him. To my son, Steven, who God has blessed with a compassionate heart and with a desire to seek after Him.

~ TABLE OF CONTENTS ~

Foreword   ix

Introduction   xi

1. Introducing a Loving God   13
2. I'm Not Worthy   21
3. I've Suffered So   29
4. Hanging in There   39
5. Releasing It to God   51
6. The Past, Present, and Future   63
7. What About Fears?   73
8. Eternal Life   87
9. Starting Over   97
10. Moving Forward With Faith   107
11. Taking Action   119
12. My Heart Speaks   133
13. Living in Blessings   141
14. Receiving Healing and Prosperity   157
15. Yes! God Loves Me!   171

~ FOREWORD ~

It is with great pleasure that I offer information regarding the author of this book. You don't have to be around Nancy very long until you recognize a deep sense of affection for Jesus and love for her fellow Christians. That same love that characterizes her relationship with the Lord is imparted to those to whom she ministers. Being privileged to read this manuscript before publishing, I can confidently encourage all who seek a deeper, more worshipful relationship with the Lord to get into this book, because the law of the Spirit is that you can't give what you don't have. But, Nancy certainly has what she has written about in this book, and you find that love and these truths being imparted unto you as you read. May God bless!

Pastor Larry Smith
Rivers of Refreshing Church
Florida

~ INTRODUCTION ~

*You and God
make a majority.*

Through the years I have come across so many Christians that feel unlovable, unworthy, or unwanted. Other Christians feel God is untouchable. They can't understand why or how they can have a personal relationship with a God who seems so distant to them. This has been my motivation to write this book, as well as the prompting of the Holy Spirit.

In these pages, I have approached the concept of God's love for us, not only through Christ's willingness to die in order to pay the penalty for our sins, but by emphasizing His walk while here on this earth. My goal is to help you sense the reality and love of Jesus Christ through the realization that He, too, experienced the same human feelings and emotions we do today. Just like all of us He experienced the good, the bad and the ugly - including happiness and joy, sadness and pain, laughter and tears - even anger. I believe that when we know that our experiences

~ INTRODUCTION ~

and our feelings are understood by God, it will help us accept the love He has for us. We will find that God is not untouchable, that He is not distant, and that He desires to have a "one on one" relationship with each of us.

The difference between knowing something in your mind and knowing it with your heart is acting on it. When, what you know reaches your heart, it affects your life. And when you act on your beliefs, you will also affect the lives of others.

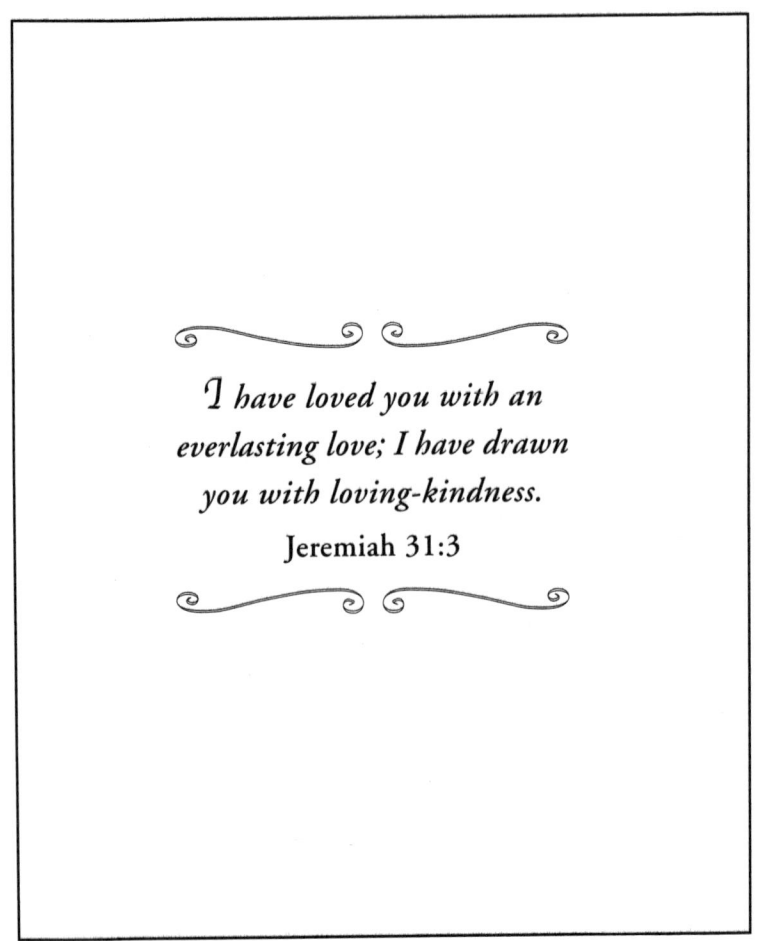

I have loved you with an everlasting love; I have drawn you with loving-kindness.

Jeremiah 31:3

~ CHAPTER ONE ~

Introducing a Loving God

Yes, "God loves you." Are these words you *hear* or do you know it in your *heart*? Maybe you haven't thought much about God's love for you. Maybe you don't really believe what the words say. Maybe you think God's love only applies to others, but not to you. Maybe you feel too unworthy and unwanted to be loved by anyone, much less God. But, that is not the case.

The Love of Our Heavenly Father

How would you feel if your Father picked you up in His arms and said to you, "I love you!" Well, just like your earthly father, your Heavenly Father is there to pick you up and tell you, "I love you."

The Psalmist tells us: "The Lord is compassionate and gracious, slow to anger, abounding in love" (Psalm 103:8).

~ CHAPTER ONE ~

Did you catch all that? He cares about your circumstances and is merciful. He is not a continually angry God. No, He is *slow* to anger. He abounds in love.

Do you remember playing the "How much do I love you" game when you were little with someone who loved you? To play the game, you stretch out your arms and say, "I love you this much." Or you say things like, "I love you as much as all the sand on the beach" or "I love you as much as all the stars in the sky." Each person trying to "outdo" the other.

Guess what? God likes that game, too: "For as high as the heavens are above the earth, so great is his love for those who fear him..." (Psalm 103:11). His love is as high as the heavens are above the earth. In Ephesians, Paul also tells us: "...to grasp how wide and long and high and deep is the love of Christ..." (Ephesians 3:18). Sounds like our childhood game, doesn't it? But, it is God talking directly to us describing the dimensions of His love. As Paul says:

> *...neither height nor depth, nor anything else in all creation, will be able to separate us from the love of God that is in Christ Jesus our Lord. (Romans 8:39)*

Throughout the Bible are infinite references to God's love for us. The Psalmist tells us: "For great is his love toward us, and the faithfulness of the Lord endures forever" (Psalm 117:2). And, then again in Psalm 118:29: "...his love endures forever." No matter what, He still loves you and wants what is best for you.

Perhaps the most familiar verse and the most powerful evidence of all, says:

> *For God so loved the world that he gave his one and only Son, that whoever believes in him shall not perish but have eternal life. (John 3:16)*

~ *Introducing a Loving God* ~

The Supreme Sacrifice of Love

God doesn't love us because we love Him – it is the other way around. We love Him because we know He loves us. Don't you usually find it much easier to love someone when you know they care about you and love you? But even more, God's love is unconditional and knows no bounds. Even in moments when we withdraw from Him, He still cares about us. In the New Testament, John gives us a clear definition of love:

> *This is love: not that we loved God, but that he loved us and sent his son as an atoning sacrifice for our sins. (I John 4:10)*

Our sins have separated us from a Holy, loving God and the penalty for those sins is death. But, God created man to have fellowship with Him. So in His infinite wisdom and mercy God planned for a way for mankind to be brought back into fellowship with Him. He would send His son, Jesus Christ, to pay the penalty of death for all men and women and then cover them with His Son's righteousness.

Yes, God was willing to send His son to die for us, so that we could have the opportunity to live with Him for eternity – "for God so loved the world." He didn't wait for us to become good or perfect or whole. Instead, Christ was willing to die for us while we were still unrepentant and unfamiliar with His ways: "But God demonstrates his own love for us in this: While we were still sinners, Christ died for us" (Romans 5:8).

God's very nature is love – that's what He is all about. Even if you were the only person on the face of the earth, God still would have sent Jesus to die for you. Jesus still would have gone through all that suffering just for you. Why? Because He loves you that much – because "God is love" (1 John 4:16).

~ CHAPTER ONE ~

You Are Special to God

In God's eyes, you are unique, special, and one of a kind. He loves you so much that He was willing to empty Himself of His former Glory and come to earth in the form of a man. After living an exemplary life, He died on a cross – bearing your sins so that He could prove how much He really does love you.

He is not a distant, uncaring God. No. Through His own personal experience, He can identify and sympathize with you. He knows what it is like to experience the hard knocks of life. Instead of indifferent and far away, He is down-to-earth, up front, and personal and has vowed to be "with you always, to the very end of the age" (Matthew 28:20) and on into eternity. That's a powerful, magnificent promise that only a loving, tender and merciful Lord could offer.

You need to know, that you know, that you *know*, how much God loves you. You *are* the daughter He has always wanted. You *are* the son He has always sought. God loves you. His love is like nothing else. Don't think to yourself, "God may love so and so, but He couldn't love *me*." He tells us that He is no respecter of persons. That means: "Yes, He can love you and He does!"

When I had my first child, I loved her so much that it was beyond expression. When I became pregnant with my second child, I wondered how it would be possible to love another child as much as I loved my first daughter. But I found I was capable of loving my second daughter just as much as my first. Then my son came along. Again more love poured out from my heart. It is in this same way that God loves us. No matter how many of us there are or will be, His love just keeps growing and growing and *growing*. He calls us His

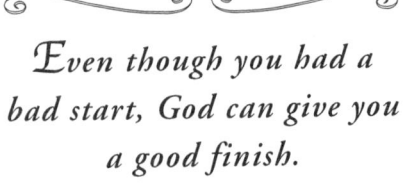

Even though you had a bad start, God can give you a good finish.

~ Introducing a Loving God ~

children. He tells us He has an abundance of love for each and every one of us. Even more, His love endures forever – it is unending.

If you have ever felt unwanted or rejected by your parents, you know what a sad and unfortunate situation it can be. But, in God's eyes you are wanted and loved – He hasn't rejected you, and He will never reject you. He says He will never leave you nor forsake you, and you can count on that! In Isaiah 49:16, God says, ". . .I will not forget you! See, I have engraved you on the palms of my hands . . ." When we can't rely on those around us, we can know without a doubt that we can always rely on our Heavenly Father.

There Is Assurance in God's Love

Yes, you can know with a certainty that God truly loves you, regardless of who you are or what you've done! Do you feel you've done too many things wrong for God to really love you? Well, you don't have to feel that way any longer. His love is unconditional. He doesn't care about where you've been or what you've done – just where you're going! Even more, you don't have to work for God's love, and you don't have to earn His approval – you already have it! You don't have to try to be accepted by God, for He welcomes you with open arms just the way you are at this very moment. Paul tells us:

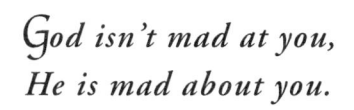

God isn't mad at you, He is mad about you.

> *For it is by grace you have been saved, through faith – and this not from yourselves, it is the gift of God – not by works, so that no one can boast. (Ephesians 2:8-9)*

~ CHAPTER ONE ~

God Understands

Do you wonder if God understands what you have been through? Maybe a faraway distant being couldn't. But, our Lord has lived and walked on this earth. In Hebrews, the writer tells us that Jesus, the Son of God – our High Priest – is able to sympathize with our weaknesses because while on this earth, He, too, experienced human suffering and temptation just like the rest of us:

> *. . .we see Jesus, who was made a little lower than the angels, now crowned with glory and honor because he suffered death, so that by the grace of God he might taste death for everyone. . .*
>
> *Since the children have flesh and blood, he too shared in their humanity so that by his death he might destroy him who holds the power of death – that is, the devil – and free those who all their lives were held in slavery by their fear of death. . . .*
>
> *For this reason he had to be made like his brothers in every way, in order that he might become a merciful and faithful high priest in service to God, and that he might make atonement for the sins of the people.*
>
> *Because he himself suffered when he was tempted, he is able to help those who are being tempted. Therefore, holy brothers, who share in the heavenly calling, fix your thoughts on Jesus, the apostle and high priest whom we confess. (Hebrews 2:9, 14-18, 3:1)*

~ Introducing a Loving God ~

Do You Feel You Have Failed?

Keep in mind that "failure" isn't always a negative word. And, if we fail, we can be taught lessons which we could not have learned otherwise. In other words, sometimes failure can be a blessing in disguise. Interestingly, the word "failure" is not found in the King James Version of the Bible and only once in the NIV where it is written as a positive, for Paul says ". . .our visit to you was not a failure" (1 Thessalonians 2:1).

The "Substance of Things Hoped For"

Yes, God loves you! And, He is not shy about telling you so! In Psalms we learn that the Lord is "compassionate and gracious. . . abounding in love" (Psalm 103:8). The Psalmist also said of the Lord: "All your words are true" (Psalm 119:160). In other words, we can depend on God, because He has set the standard for truth! But, first He expects us to have faith in Him. Having faith involves action. When we believe God and trust in His word, our faith will cause us to think differently, to speak differently, and to act differently. Faith is not abstract – it is real. It is "the substance of things hoped for, the evidence of things not seen" (Hebrews 11:1 KJV).

You can never get so low that it is too low for God.

Getting to Know the God Who Loves You

The Creator of this universe cherishes you. He has set His affection on you. Psalm 149:4 says He "delights" in you. God's love created you and it saved you. His love will guide you and He will listen to you no matter where you are – no matter what state of mind you are in. No one knows you like God does, and no one will ever love you like He can.

~ CHAPTER ONE ~

In the pages of this book, we'll be covering the following questions and so much more – together.

- *Would you rather trust in yourself or the God Who created you?*

- *Would you rather depend on yourself or in God who can make all things possible?*

- *Would you rather fight your own battles or let God fight them for you?*

- *Would you rather struggle to climb the "ladder" of life or let God promote you?*

Now, come along while we explore the depth and dimension of God's love for you, how you can know for a certainty that He loves you, and how you, in turn, can show God just how much you love and appreciate Him!

~ CHAPTER TWO ~

I'm Not Worthy

Do you think you've done too many things wrong for God to really love you? You haven't. Paul states: "for all have sinned and fall short of the glory of God" (Romans 3:23). So you see, we are all in the same boat. The disciple James pronounced: "For whoever keeps the whole law and yet stumbles at just one point is guilty of breaking all of it" (James 2:10). Since the law is the expression of God's character and will, when we disregard one part of the law, we disregard God's will. As a result, we violate His whole law.

David's Example

The life of David is a good example for us. Even though he didn't lead a sinless life, David is still the most honored man in scripture next to Christ. He's mentioned 1,100 times in the Bible and is called "a man after God's own heart." David was found to be a man with a grateful heart. The book of Psalms – which contains much of his writings – is filled with gratefulness, praise, and the giving of thanks to God.

As a boy, David was anointed to be king by Samuel the Prophet. Years later, after the death of King Saul, David became King of Israel. He was a man that served and loved God. But, he wasn't perfect and he fell prey to his own desires and not only committed adultery, but also had an innocent man murdered. Fortunately, he became convicted in his soul of his sins and repented before God. He still had to pay the consequences for his actions. But, because he was willing to turn back to God, the Lord was merciful and forgiving:

> *If we confess our sins, he is faithful and just and will forgive us our sins and purify us from all unrighteousness. (I John 1:9)*

You Are Forgiven

It is through Jesus that we receive forgiveness of sins. But did you know, repenting is more than just saying, "I'm sorry." True repentance means turning away from your sins by no longer continuing in them. It's making a *radical change* in your life. We also need to acknowledge Jesus as our Savior because He was the One who paid the penalty for our sins – and that penalty was death. Since Christ died in your place, you no longer have to pay for that debt. You have been pardoned, and as a result, you are forgiven. In Acts, Peter told the crowd:

> *Repent and be baptized every one of you, in the name of Jesus Christ for the forgiveness of your sins. And you will receive the gift of the Holy Spirit. (Acts 2:38)*

~ I'm Not Worthy ~

You Are Righteous

Christ's blood has caused us to be covered with His righteousness: "This righteousness from God comes through faith in Jesus Christ to all who believe. . ." (Romans 3:22). Isn't this wonderful? Now we no longer have to go around putting ourselves down and feeling guilty! Paul tells us: ". . . there is now no condemnation for those who are in Christ Jesus" (Romans 8:1). Why? Because "through Christ Jesus the law of the Spirit of life set me free from the law of sin and death" (Romans 8:2). Since Christ was victorious over sin and kept the law without fault, you now have the ability to keep it without fault – since He lives in you through the Holy Spirit. And, because Christ took your place on the cross, you no longer have to pay the penalty of death for your past sins.

Continuing in Romans, Paul clarifies for us that those who are controlled by the Spirit of Christ that lives in them will no longer live according to the sinful nature. Instead, they will live according to the Spirit: "You, however, are controlled not by the sinful nature but by the Spirit, if the Spirit of God lives in you" (Romans 8:9).

And, when you are tempted to sin, remember the warning in James:

> *When tempted, no one should say, 'God is tempting me.' For God cannot be tempted by evil, nor does he tempt anyone; but each one is tempted when, by his own evil desire, he is dragged away and enticed. (James 1:13-14).*

Salvation Is Yours

Jesus has bought salvation for you. You have been reconciled to God through the sacrifice and blood of Christ. Paul tells us:

~ CHAPTER TWO ~

For God did not appoint us to suffer wrath but to receive salvation through our Lord Jesus Christ. (1 Thessalonians 5:9)

From the Psalmist, we learn: "as far as the east is from the west, so far has He removed our transgressions from us" (Psalm 103:12). Do you know how far the east is from the west? They are so far apart that they never meet. In God's eyes, your past no longer exists. God isn't holding anything against you – your debts have been canceled. Paul sums it for us:

Therefore, if anyone is in Christ, he is a new creation; the old has gone, the new has come! All this is from God, who reconciled us to Himself through Christ . . . not counting men's sins against them. Be reconciled to God. God made Him who had no sin to be sin for us, so that in Him we might become the righteousness of God. (2 Corinthians 5:17-21)

A Parable From the Vineyard

In Matthew 20:1-16, we find the parable of the workers in the vineyard. In this parable, Jesus makes an analogy between the Kingdom of Heaven and a landowner who went out early in the day to hire men to work in his vineyard. This landowner agreed to pay those he hired that morning a certain amount for their work and sent them into the vineyard.

It doesn't matter where you are coming from, only where you are going.

Throughout the day, the landowner continued to make several trips to the market place and hire workers for his vineyard. In the evening, the owner had his foreman call the workers and pay them their wages. The workers that arrived later throughout the day were paid the *same wage* as the workers that started early in the morning. Those who had done most of the work – and in the heat of the day – became upset because the new workers had received the same compensation, but for less effort.

As I was reading this parable, I thought to myself, "That really is unfair. Their wage should have been based on how long they worked." As I continued reading this parable, I began to understand. When the workers complained about this seemingly unfair practice, the owner reminded them that they had contracted for that specific amount. Why, then, should they be upset if he paid the others the same amount, even if it was for less work? The owner of the vineyard went on to explain that if he wanted to give the man that was hired later in the day the same wage as he had given the one hired earlier, it shouldn't be any concern of theirs. He then responded to the complainers with this question:

> *Don't I have the right to do what I want with my own money? Or are you envious because I am generous?' (Matthew 20:15)*

When we compare the vineyard in this parable to the Kingdom of Heaven, we see that those who spent their whole life serving God and those who come to accept Him later in life – or even those who accepted Him on their death bed – all receive *equally* the salvation of God and eternity with Him. By this parable, we see that it is never too late to have a relationship with the Lord. Salvation is not based on works. It is based solely on God's overwhelming generosity. His grace is undeniable. In *all* His ways, He is holy, just, loving, and righteous.

You Are Accepted

God wants us to know His love is unconditional. We don't have to work for His love. As we walk with the Lord and

~ CHAPTER TWO ~

because He loves us, we find He has a way of revealing to us the areas in our life we need to work on to become more and more the person He intends for us to be. Here is an example from my own life. At one time I would have said, "No, I don't have a competitive nature," but God revealed to me that I did. He brought to my awareness how I was always striving to be the best or better than someone else. At first I thought, there is nothing wrong in that because God wants us to do our best – right? I even found a scripture to back me up:

> *Whatever you do, work at it with all your heart, as working for the Lord, not for men, since you know that you will receive an inheritance from the Lord as a reward. It is the Lord Christ you are serving. (Colossians 3:23-24)*

Yes, the verse was true, but my application of it was wrong. Without realizing it, I had been striving for approval in order to still my feelings of inadequacy and inferiority. And sometimes, I was striving out of jealousy. Instead, I should have been doing my best for the Lord, and because I wanted to become all God wanted me to be. I came to understand that God looks at the heart – at our attitude and our motives. He wants a pure heart – one that is not selfish. We learn in Proverbs: "All a man's ways seem innocent to him, but motives are weighed by the Lord" (Proverbs 16:2). The Lord taught me that I didn't have to be striving for something He already had given me.

And, you don't have to feel as if you always need to be striving – for whatever reason: whether it be for a sense of worth, for approval, for love or for acceptance. God has already placed His seal of approval on you. God tells you He will remember your sins no more. You don't have to try to be accepted. You are already accepted by the most important person in the world – your Creator.

~ *I'm Not Worthy* ~

You Are Valuable

How much are you worth in the eyes of God? Jesus thought you were worth dying for! His words *spoke* of His love, but His sacrificial death *showed* His love. Jesus' own words tell us: "Greater love has no one than this, that he lay down his life for his friends" (John 15:13). Even though you may feel or may have felt that you are not worth very much, it's not up to you to decide what your value is. You are valuable and you are worthy – because *God* has said you are.

He loves us with an everlasting love. Each one of us is that special son or daughter He always wanted. Realize how special you are. When you do, you will *act* special. Remember, to God, you are *wonderful*, you are *beautiful*, and you are *precious*. That is how He sees you.

Isaiah has said: "Yet, O Lord, you are our Father. We are the clay, you are the potter; we are all the work of your hand" (Isaiah 64:8). Yes, God has started the process of salvation in you and He will continue it until it is brought to completion. Paul tells us:

> . . .being confident of this, that he who began a good work in you will carry it on to completion until the day of Christ Jesus. (Philippians 1:6)

God is so wonderful. His love is everlasting. In Jeremiah, God tells us: ". . . I have loved you with an everlasting love; I have drawn you with lovingkindness" (Jeremiah 31:3). And then Paul, in Romans 8:39, says that "*nothing*" in all creation can separate us from the love of God. In Christ Jesus, we have so many reasons to be thankful.

We are a designer's original, a product of God's creativity.

~ CHAPTER THREE ~

I've Suffered So

Does God seem distant and far away? Do you sometimes find yourself thinking: "If God really loved me, He wouldn't let me suffer so?" Do you think He is unable to relate to what you are experiencing? Or, maybe you think He just doesn't care. Do you sometimes ask:

> *"Where is God?"*
>
> *"Why isn't He intervening?"*
>
> *"Why am I going through this?"*
>
> *"Why? Why? Why?"*

In Hebrews, the writer tells us that Jesus, the Son of God – our High Priest – is able to sympathize with our weaknesses.

~ CHAPTER THREE ~

How? Because, while on this earth, He also experienced human suffering and human temptation:

> *For we do not have a high priest who is unable to sympathize with our weaknesses, but we have one who has been tempted in every way, just as we are – yet was without sin. (Hebrews 4:15)*

Jesus was a pure, spotless, blameless sacrifice for your sins and for mine – for all those who would call upon His Name. Yet Isaiah prophesied that Jesus would be "... despised and rejected by men, a man of sorrows, and familiar with suffering. . ." (Isaiah 53:3).

How Can He *Really* Understand?

Do you think God could never understand what you have been through or what you are presently going through? Let's find out!

Have You Lost a Loved One?

Jesus understands because He lost loved ones, too. History tells us He lost his earthly father at an early age. As the oldest, He also had the added responsibility of helping to raise his brothers and sisters.

As a young man, Jesus lost His cousin and good friend, John the Baptist, to a horrendous and untimely death. Jesus and John were close in age and grew up together, sharing in all the activities that two best friends would. After they were grown, John prepared the way for Jesus' ministry. Then, suddenly by violent hands, John was gone. When Jesus heard the news that John had been beheaded, He wanted to be alone. So He went off by himself to a remote area to mourn the loss of His beloved friend and relative. Yes, Jesus understands your loss.

~ I've Suffered So ~

Have You Lost a Child?

Maybe you cried out to God: "Where were you?" But, did you hear God softly reply, "I was in the same place that I was when my Son Jesus died." Yes, your Heavenly Father knows your pain.

Have You Felt Unappreciated?

Maybe you didn't get the recognition you deserved after "going the extra mile." During a trip to Jerusalem, ten men who had leprosy met Jesus along the way. Standing at a distance, they called out to Him. Responding, Jesus cleansed them of their disease. But, only one, out of all those men, came back to say, "Thank you" after they were healed. The other ungrateful men went on their way without so much as a backward glance:

> Jesus asked 'Were not all ten cleansed? Where are the other nine? Was no one found to return and give praise to God except this foreigner?' (Luke 17:17-18)

Yes, Jesus understands how you feel.

Have You Felt Misunderstood?

When Jesus asked His disciples:

> ...'Who do people say I am?' They replied, 'Some say John the Baptist; others say Elijah; and still others, one of the prophets'... he asked, 'Who do you say I am?' Peter answered, 'You are the Christ.' (Mark 8:27-29)

~ CHAPTER THREE ~

At that time few people realized who Jesus was or even why He was on this earth. Some even laughed at Him, ridiculed Him, and eventually had Him crucified without ever knowing that He was the Son of God – their Savior – Who had come in order to save them. Yes, Jesus understands what it's like to be misunderstood.

Has Someone Made Fun of You?

After the soldiers led Jesus away, they put a purple robe on Him and a "crown" of thorns on His head. They mocked Him, shouting, "Hail, king of the Jews" (Mark 15:18). You can imagine how they made fun of Him, saying, "Some king – look at you now!"

These foolish men dared to mock Christ's deity by pretending to worship Him: ". . . Falling on their knees, they paid homage to him" (Mark 15:19). They treated Jesus in the most contemptuous manner imaginable. Yes, Jesus knows what it's like to be made fun of by others.

Have People Told Lies About You?

In Mark 14:55-56, we find that the Sanhedrin and chief priests were looking for evidence against Jesus. They wanted an excuse to put Him to death, but they couldn't find one. This passage tells us: "Many testified falsely against him, but their statements did not agree." Yes, Jesus understands what it's like to be falsely accused.

Have You Felt Betrayed by a Close Friend?

As Jesus was eating with His disciples, He told them: ". . . I tell you the truth, one of you will betray me – one who is eating with me" (Mark 14:18). Jesus was referring to Judas Iscariot. Judas had conspired with the Jewish hierarchy to betray Jesus and turn Him over to them. Here was one of the

~ I've Suffered So ~

chosen – one of the elite twelve disciples who had been hand-picked by Jesus Himself – who had sat at the feet of Christ, ate with Him, and listened to His teachings. Yet he betrayed Him for a little financial gain:

> *Then one of the Twelve – the one called Judas Iscariot – went to the chief priests and asked, 'What are you willing to give me if I hand him over to you?' So they counted out for him thirty silver coins. From then on Judas watched for an opportunity to hand him over. (Matthew 26:14-16)*

The equivalent in our monetary system today would be a laborer's wage for six months. How do you think Jesus must have felt, knowing his so-called friend and disciple thought that was all his life was worth.

After Jesus was seized and arrested, the other disciples fled the scene, leaving their Master in His time of greatest need: "Then everyone deserted him and fled" (Mark 14:50). These men had been at His side day after day – they were His best friends! Yes, Jesus knows how it feels to be betrayed.

Have You Suffered Physical Abuse?

We know Jesus went about teaching and healing the sick. We also know He did no wrong and never sinned. But the Sanhedrin, the Jewish supreme court of His day, and the high priest accused Jesus of blasphemy because of His teachings. Mark recounts:

> *... They all condemned him as worthy of death. Then some began to spit at him; they blindfolded him, struck him with their fists ... And the guards took him and beat him. (Mark 14:64-65)*

~ CHAPTER THREE ~

What a horrible picture! But that wasn't the worst of it. Later, Pilate, who was an officer of the Roman Empire and controlled the province of Judaea, also had Jesus whipped and beaten and then sentenced Him to death: "Wanting to satisfy the crowd, Pilate . . . had Jesus flogged, and handed Him over to be crucified (Mark 15:15).

The soldiers led Jesus away, then proceeded to twist together a makeshift "crown" of razor-sharp thorns and set it on His forehead, making Him bleed profusely. Again and again, they struck Him on the head with a staff and spit on Him. Then, they marched Him out of town to be crucified, carrying the weight of a massive wooden cross on His shoulders during the long trek to Golgotha.

Why – why would He allow this to happen? Isaiah tells us:

> *. . . he was pierced for our transgressions, he was crushed for our iniquities; the punishment that brought us peace was upon him, and by his wounds we are healed. (Isaiah 53:5)*

Yes, Jesus knows what it's like to be abused.

Have You Felt Rejected by Someone You Loved?

As Jesus was hanging on the cross, dying, Mark tells us:

> *And at the ninth hour Jesus cried out in a loud voice. . . 'My God, my God, why have you forsaken me?' (Mark 15:34)*

Our sins separate us from God. Because of those sins, He must "hide His face" or turn His back towards us. Isaiah tells us: ". . .your iniquities have separated you from your God; your sins have hidden His face from you, so that He will not hear" (Isaiah 59:2). Then, in a letter to the Corinthians, Paul wrote:

~ I've Suffered So ~

> *God made him [Jesus] who had no sin to be sin for us, so that in him we might become the righteousness of God (2 Corinthians 5:21, Comment in brackets added)*

Therefore, when Jesus was placed on the cross, all our sins were put on *His* head, and God the Father had to turn His back towards Jesus and look away. At that moment, when Jesus carried the sins of this world, He experienced the ultimate loneliness. He felt the ultimate rejection. Yes, Jesus understands.

Yes, He Understands

Jesus can understand what you are feeling. He can understand what you are going through or have gone through. He is full of compassion and is able to comfort you because He also suffered. Now, because He knows what it is like to suffer these things, He is always interceding for us before our Heavenly Father: ". . . Christ Jesus. . . is at the right hand of God and is also interceding for us" (Romans 8:34). Paul praises God for His compassion and comfort:

> *Praise be to the God and Father of our Lord Jesus Christ, the Father of compassion and the God of all comfort, who comforts us in all our troubles, so that we can comfort those in any trouble with the comfort we ourselves have received from God. (2 Corinthians 1:3-4)*

Life's Trials

Even though we don't want to experience difficulties and pain in our life, the Bible tells us there are benefits in having to go through some troubling times:

~ CHAPTER THREE ~

> *Consider it pure joy . . . whenever you face trials of many kinds, because you know that the testing of your faith develops perseverance. Perseverance must finish its work so that you may be mature and complete, not lacking anything. (James 1:2-4)*

Realistically, we know that everything can't always be "wonderful." Although, it would be nice if this were so. Sometimes, it even seems like everything is going wrong. At that time, more than ever, we need to remind ourselves that God is in control. He takes our bad times and turns them into something good to be used for His purpose. We know that "in all things God works for the good of those who love him, who have been called according to his purpose" (Romans 8:28).

A lesson from the teakettle – it is always up to its neck in hot water, yet it still sings.

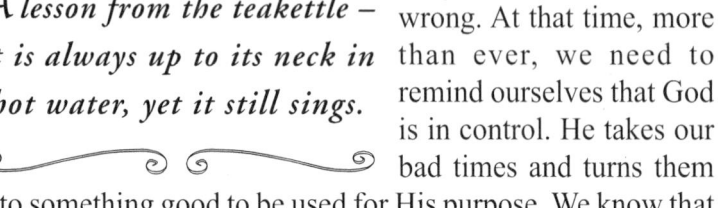

Paul stresses that there is no trial that can separate us from Jesus' love and that through Him we will always come out the victor:

> *Who shall separate us from the love of Christ? Shall trouble or hardship or persecution or famine or nakedness or danger or sword?. . . No, in all these things we are more than conquerors through him who loved us. (Romans 8:35, 37)*

We need to remember who we are and who we belong to: "You are not your own; you were bought at a price. . ." (1 Corinthians 6:19-20). That price was the life and blood of Jesus Christ. As believers we are ". . . a chosen people, a royal priesthood, a holy nation, a people belonging to God. . ." (1 Peter 2:9). James, the brother of Jesus, tells us:

~ I've Suffered So ~

Blessed is the man who perseveres under trial, because when he has stood the test, he will receive the crown of life that God has promised to those who love him. (James 1:12)

It also helps to remember James 5:13, 16 which says: "Is any one of you in trouble? He should pray. . ." and that ". . .The prayer of a righteous man is powerful and effective." David also encourages us to turn to God in prayer: "The righteous cry out, and the Lord hears them; he delivers them from all their troubles" (Psalms 34:17).

We are victors, not victims.

Extending God's Love

There was a time when I focused on all the problems and troubles in my life. Instead of giving them to the Lord, I wallowed in pity, feeling sorry for myself. Instead of being filled with a joy that comes from knowing God and who I am in Him, I continually concentrated on my own misery. As a result, I was always miserable. "Woe is me" became my "signature" phrase. I continually thought and spoke negatively about my life.

Did you know it has been found that negative thoughts, in thirty seconds, can cause over two hundred and fifty chemical reactions in your body. It then takes forty-eight hours to work these out of your system. No wonder when I was in a negative mode, I felt so badly.

Well, one day my young son came to me and said, "Mom, all you ever say is 'Woe is me' and I'm tired of hearing it." Listening to him say it back to me made me realize how it really sounded. I also realized that I was reinforcing the negative in my life by speaking that way.

~ CHAPTER THREE ~

At that very moment I decided my life would change and "Woe is me" would no longer be part of my vocabulary. Yes, I can gratefully announce that my life did begin changing for the better – but it was a process, one which required a brand new attitude on my part in order to begin. That change in attitude involved giving God my past and trusting Him with my future.

It is so true that God can give you the power and strength to walk through or over or around those things that come against you. Remember: "I can do everything through him [Christ] who gives me strength" (Philippians 4:13, Comments in brackets added). And, remember ". . . all things are possible with God" (Mark 10:27).

One of the lessons you can learn through suffering is compassion for others. The trials in your own life often help you to better understand what others are going through. Through your own suffering, you become more equipped to help others. Then, you can take the comfort and love God has given you and extend it to them.

> *Nothing can happen that you and God can't handle together.*

~ CHAPTER FOUR ~

Hanging in There

We hear a lot about success and failure these days, but did you know "failure" isn't always a negative word? When we fail, we can be taught lessons which we could not have learned otherwise. Often, failures turn out to be blessings in disguise. They are good learning experiences. Through failure, we can learn from our mistakes, as well as learning to have patience and motivation to keep trying. In other words, sometimes we just have to *hang in there* and not be so quick to give up!

Turning Failure Into Success

Here is a good illustration. In the game of baseball, do you know who "struck out" more times than anyone else in his day? Would you believe it was none other than Babe Ruth – the man who was known as the *Home Run King!* He hit more

~ CHAPTER FOUR ~

home runs than anyone else – 715 to be exact. But he also struck out 1,330 times!

Through the years since the time of "the Babe," most people have forgotten how many times he struck out. Instead, they remember that Babe Ruth was one of the all-time great hitters in the history of baseball. From this, you can see how people are usually remembered more often for their accomplishments rather than for their mistakes.

> *Success is never ending, and failure is never final.*

The Writer Who Overcame Rejection

Another good illustration is a well-known author who became one of the best-selling novelists in modern literary history, with more than one hundred books in print. But, before he became a success, this man had left high school to strike out on his own. He spent fifteen years working at odd jobs and as a merchant seaman. When he first started writing, he received hundreds of rejections before finally getting published. This man was Louis L'Amour.

Now, his 100+ books have been translated into twenty-six languages and more than forty-five of his novels have been made into feature films and television movies. Among other notable accomplishments, he became the first novelist to be awarded the *Congressional Gold Medal* by the U.S. Congress in honor of his life's work!

A "Doodler" Who Changed the World

Here's another good illustration. Because of his love for writing, this man wrote a series of fairy tales. Unfortunately, they just didn't sell. He finally landed a job with a newspaper. But, not too long after starting the job, the paper's editor fired

~ Hanging in There ~

him, claiming he didn't have any good ideas to contribute and had a habit of doodling too much. The editor didn't hesitate to tell him that he didn't have any talent.

Who was he? It was Walt Disney! His "doodling" led to the creation of Mickey Mouse, Donald Duck, Goofy, Pluto and all the gang! Walt Disney went on to build the most famous theme parks in all the world – Disneyland and Walt Disney World. Even more astounding, he won worldwide acclaim and became the winner of forty-five academy awards.

The Inventor Who Never Gave Up

Here's another famous example. Teachers called this little boy slow and too stupid to learn. All he had was three months of schooling, but his undaunted mother taught him herself at home. By the age of ten, he was reading on a college level and had built a chemistry lab in his basement. There, he had *thousands* of failures before perfecting his invention – the light bulb!

Do you know who he is? Of course, it was Thomas Edison! Mr. Edison went on to create and develop over 1300 inventions and eventually held 1093 patents. But there are two success stories here – a mother who wouldn't give up and a boy willing to learn even when faced with overwhelming difficulties.

The Man Who Would Be President

Here is yet another great example. This man was said to have no future at all. He came from a poor family and had little encouragement to succeed. In fact, he failed several times in business, was defeated when he ran for the Legislature, had a nervous breakdown, and again suffered defeat when he ran for the Senate and the Vice Presidency. In all, he lost twenty-three elections while winning only three.

Do you know who this is? It is the man who's greatest victory came in 1860 when he was elected President of the

~ CHAPTER FOUR ~

United States of America. That man was Abraham Lincoln, who went on to become one of our nation's greatest presidents. Even though President Lincoln had more failures than most, he was never really defeated because he never stopped trying. He was definitely a man with perseverance and determination.

The Lady Who Went All the Way to Hollywood

Here's another good one. At age fifteen, this young girl went to New York and attended drama school, but was unsuccessful in obtaining any kind of role on Broadway. She paid her rent by making sodas in a Manhattan drugstore. At age seventeen, she was stricken with rheumatoid arthritis and was practically paralyzed for two years.

At age twenty-two, she went to Hollywood and began a slow rise in a string of second-rate movies. One director told her to go home because she would never make it as a professional actor. She was told she would never be a star. Eventually, she was approached by CBS to do a television show. She requested her husband be her co-star. The network insisted the public wouldn't accept them as a couple, so they formed their own company. They worked up a variety act and went on tour.

After a sensational response, CBS reconsidered and offered to do a pilot show. Even though they received many rejections, they finally found a sponsor. Do you know who they were? Would you believe Lucille Ball and Desi Arnez! The show was called, "I Love Lucy!"

You Can Never Be Defeated if You Never Give Up!

These are just a few of the famous people in history who didn't let failure stop them. In fact, they went on to turn their failure into success. What did all these people have in common?

~ Hanging in There ~

~ *They had an idea, a goal, or a vision.*

~ *They took chances again and again.*

~ *They took their failures in stride and kept on trying.*

~ *They were people who didn't give up.*

~ *They made mistakes, but they learned from them.*

Don't let the fear of failure prevent you from achieving. Remember, you have to take chances in order to have great success. In other words – you can never be defeated if you never stop trying.

Trusting in the Lord

Wouldn't we all like to live without problems? Unfortunately, it won't ever be that way. Problems and trials are just a part of this life. But, you don't have to let the cares of this world overwhelm and crush you. If you view adversity or handicaps as a challenge and don't give up, you will eventually succeed. God has a purpose for your life. The comforting words of Jeremiah tell us so:

> *'For I know the plans I have for you,' declares the Lord, 'plans to prosper you and not to harm you, plans to give you hope and a future. (Jeremiah 29:11)*

Troubles are a part of life and that's just a fact. But, they don't have to separate you from God. Remember who God is, and it will change your perspective. He has the ability to

~ CHAPTER FOUR ~

change the situation. And, if He doesn't change the situation, He gives you the strength to go through it – to "weather the storm." Let God do the worrying for you. Let God take control of the situation. Then, focus on the goal – not the circumstance. Keep in mind, hard times will pass away. They are not here to stay.

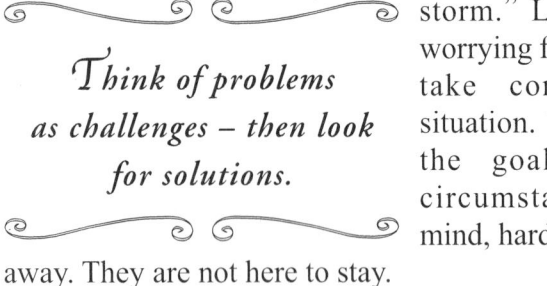

> *Think of problems as challenges – then look for solutions.*

The Bible encourages you to: "Commit to the Lord whatever you do, and your plans will succeed" (Proverbs 16:3). Also:

> *Trust in the Lord with all your heart and lean not on your own understanding; in all your ways acknowledge him, and he will make your paths straight. (Proverbs 3:5-6)*

We acknowledge our Lord by serving Him with a willing and faithful heart. He makes our path straight by removing the obstacles from our pathway and taking us to our goal. He will also take the bad circumstances and situations and make something good come from them – even if it is a lesson learned.

God Will See You Through

Have you ever put off something really important you felt called to do because you were waiting for all your problems to be solved and everything to be perfect? But, time and again, as soon as you solved the problems, new ones would arise? As a result, you ended up not accomplishing anything? The Bible teaches us to set our priorities and then step out on faith into the place God wants us to be. Paul wrote: "I can do everything through him [Jesus] who gives me strength" (Philippians 4:13, Comments in brackets added).

~ Hanging in There ~

Years ago, God placed the desire on my heart to lead Bible studies in my home. I was so excited when our church started a program for women's study groups. But, for the first few years, I couldn't think of doing any more than being a participant. I felt I had too many problems in my personal life to resolve, including both marital and physical ones. In other words, I was looking for the perfect circumstances before I would step out into the place I felt God calling me to.

With the Holy Spirit continuing to prompt me, I finally decided to have a women's study group in our home. Unexpectedly, I received a call asking if I would be the hostess, so another woman, who wasn't able to use her home, could come in to lead the group. Initially, I felt disappointed. But, God loves to bless and I found myself receiving a lot of inner healing through her prayers during that time. I also witnessed more of the power of the Holy Spirit as He worked through her. It turned out to be a time of continual growing and preparation time for me. This worked out nicely for awhile. But, God was tugging at my heart to do more. Soon, I felt like a race horse that had been held back, anxiously wanting to break forth into that winning run. I was determined not to put the desire God placed in my heart on the back burner again.

That next year I was anointed for the Women's Ministry and lead a women's study group. The circumstances of my life were not perfect, although there was a sense of peace in doing what I knew I was suppose to do.

Be aware that we have an enemy that puts the heat on when we are in God's will. My marriage began going downhill again. I fell into a deep depression. Getting up became an effort. Going to work became an effort. Just moving became an effort. I'd pray and ask God why living had to be so difficult. As a result of the depression, I became incapable of continuing to lead the Bible study group.

I began to feel guilty for letting my group down – especially my co-leader, even though she was very capable of taking over when I wasn't there. Most of all, I felt guilty for letting

~ CHAPTER FOUR ~

God down. All I could think about at the time was being able to get through work so I could go home to bed.

There was one special lady in particular who wasn't willing to let me rest in that dark hole I found myself in, with the darkness continuing to press in on me. She prayed for me and with me. She encouraged me in so many ways. Thankfully, I soon learned that I had clinical depression. I learned that being depressed and being in a depression are totally different. Clinical depression results in a chemical imbalance in the brain. It takes medication or a miracle of healing from God to come out of it. It isn't something you can talk yourself out of or be talked out of. Unless you've endured depression, you can't realize how black and devastating it is to your feelings and emotions. Finally, through medication and the wonderful prayers of this faithful friend, I was healed.

Another friend at that time received the brunt of my marital complaints. You know, God places certain people in our lives for a reason. I'm not a fighter. I don't like confrontation. I'd rather say, "It's not working – I'm out of here." This friend was my "Rock of Gibralter" and encouraged me to face the challenge instead of running from it. There were many others who prayed for me during those times. I'm thankful to each of them. What James tells us regarding prayer is so true: ". . . The prayer of a righteous man *is* powerful and effective" (James 5:16).

No matter what you go through, remember that everything is temporary and will pass. The light in the darkness is the love of God. The Psalmist reminds us that: "God is our refuge and strength, an ever-present help in trouble" (Psalm 46:1). Hold unto this great promise. God *will* see you through.

Putting on Your Armor

Satan doesn't want to see us serve the Lord. He doesn't want us to fulfill our destiny. He is jealous over the fact that we were created in the image of God, so he wars against us,

~ Hanging in There ~

constantly finding the back roads and inroads into our lives – to discourage us and put us down. We must always be vigilant:

> *For our struggle is not against flesh and blood, but against the rulers, against the authorities, against the powers of this dark world and against the spiritual forces of evil in the heavenly realms. (Ephesians 6:12)*

God wants you to know that, ". . . the one who is in you [Jesus Christ by the Holy Spirit] is greater than the one [Satan] who is in the world" (1 John 4:4, Comments in brackets added). Plus, God has given you everything you need to fight the devil, Satan, and win. Paul says:

> *Finally, be strong in the Lord and in his mighty power. Put on the full armor of God so that you can take your stand against the devil's schemes. (Ephesians 6:10-11)*

To be strong in the Lord and in His power is to depend on God to be your strength and to fight for you. Continuing in Ephesians 6:13-18, you'll find all the parts of our spiritual "armor" listed. Come to the place in your walk with the Lord, where you can easily adorn yourself with the full armor of God. It includes standing your ground, then, being dressed with the belt of truth, the breastplate of righteousness with feet fitted for readiness that comes from the gospel of peace, having the shield of faith, the helmet of salvation, and the sword of the Spirit which is God's word. And, all this is to be followed by prayer.

When we stand against Satan and stand our ground, we are maintaining the position we have in Jesus Christ. We stand firm against what Satan throws at us, and we stand firm against his temptations that would draw us away from serving God. We can stand in the security of knowing Jesus' and the Father's love.

~ CHAPTER FOUR ~

Armor was defensive coverings that were worn by men going into battle to give them protection from the attacks of their enemy. Putting on the armor of God gives us protection from the attacks of our spiritual enemies. When we put on the full armor of God, we are actually clothing ourselves with His character. This is our protective covering from evil. In Romans, Paul tells us to: . . . clothe yourselves with the Lord Jesus Christ. . . (Romans 13:14). The armor is a symbolic way of saying, "Put on Christ." We are putting on the same wardrobe that He wears.

Do you have your armor on? The armor of truthfulness, righteousness, peace, faithfulness, salvation, and God's word deep in your heart? Knowing that the battle is spiritual, we also need to stay close to God in prayer, depending on Him for His help.

The greatest threat to Satan is people who are Christ-like. And, by the Holy Spirit's power, we are growing up to be just like Him. You can holler all you want at the enemy, but if you're not acting like Jesus, it won't even affect him. Holiness threatens the enemy, and love threatens him.

Paul wrote, "I have fought the good fight, I have finished the race, I have kept the faith" (2 Timothy 4:5). As Pastor David Hess said, " It's only a good fight if you win it. And God has placed you in the midst of a battle that He says you are going to win." Yes, God has given us all the armor we need, plus His power which is at work in us. We don't have to be afraid of Satan's plans against us, because God has His own plans for us – plans to give us hope and a future.

On to Victory!

Through all my trials, I have concluded that life is a series of surprises and challenges. It doesn't seem to be quite what we expect or what we want it to be. Still, no matter what, love the Lord with all your heart, trust Him and "lean not on your own understanding" (Proverbs 3:5). He will give you the

~ *Hanging in There* ~

strength to endure and conquer the trials of life – even when you think you can't, because He can! He is a good God. Even though at times life is tough, remember this life is only temporary. We have eternity in His love and presence to look forward to.

God has a plan for each of us. He's given us hope and a future. We have to look where we are going, not where we have been. He gives us strength to overcome and gives us – both you and me – the *victory!*

*Work for the Lord –
His retirement plan is
out of this world!*

~ CHAPTER FIVE ~

Releasing It to God

When we love someone we don't like to see them hurting – physically or emotionally. God is the same way. If you have a need, let the healing power of God mend your inner hurts and emotions. God is able. He is our deliverer. He is our healer. I am so glad God is in the healing business, aren't you? He is the healer, not only of our bodies, but also of our minds, our emotions and our relationships. The Psalmist proclaims: "He heals the brokenhearted and binds up their wounds" (Psalm 147:3). He gives us peace when we give everything over to Him.

Holding On To Pain – It's Not a Good Thing

A younger woman, from a group I attended, shared with me her pain and anger caused by her husband's violent physical abuse. Even though God was dealing with her husband, and

~ CHAPTER FIVE ~

he was beginning to overcome those violent attacks, she still found releasing her deep-seated hurts almost impossible. I was prompted to write her about how my past experiences of verbal and physical abuse from a previous relationship had affected me.

I gave her my written testimony, hoping it would encourage her by knowing she wasn't alone in her sufferings and responses. She later confided in me how much my writing to her had helped her – just by seeing her own inner pain that had been bottled inside her for so long, expressed in words. She went on to relate how encouraged she had been by knowing there was someone else who understood her situation and that there would eventually come a time when she would finally be able to release those painful emotions.

There are so many women and men who have suffered in a similar manner. The ones who are still suffering these offenses of physical and verbal abuse need our continual prayers and compassion.

The following is what I wrote:

> *Oh, the anger and the pain – the hate, the bitterness that overwhelms my whole being. See what he has done to me. Look and see and feel the pain and sadness he has brought into my life. The frustration envelops me, the anger grows like its own being inside of me until I feel I will burst. How I want to run away and hide – to be alone to lick my wounds. My soul cries out to God. Save me from such undeserved treatment. Does God hear me? Where is He?*
>
> *I cannot shake this anger. It lingers on and on – year after year – eating away at my heart. Who says, "forgive?" How can you know what I've suffered? I laugh in their faces. He deserves my anger. He deserves my hate. God*

~ Releasing It to God ~

should curse him. I ask God to let His revenge fall upon him.

Now he is gone. But wait, where is the peace? The anger, the pain, the bitterness – all rage on. Forgive? It sounds so foreign. Is that a word I'm suppose to know?

The flesh heals quickly. But, my heart continues to bleed and my soul continues to weep. Will healing ever come? The anger eats away at me like a cancer. My body is sick; my mind is sick. Help me Lord! Where is your peace? Forgive. I don't want to forgive. He doesn't deserve forgiveness. Look and see what he's done. See the pain he has caused in my heart. Forgive? He's not even sorry. He feels no regret. He doesn't seek my forgiveness. Hate overwhelms me. Lord, it hurts to hate so much.

Time goes on. It doesn't heal the memories. I bury the anger. I hide the pain. But like a snake ready to attack, it rises to lash out, its venom poisoning my soul.

Lord, I need your forgiveness. Forgive me for hanging on to this anger that embitters me. It keeps me far from you. I miss feeling your closeness. Prayer is not easy in the midst of such hatred and anger. But, I find an odd sense of satisfaction by holding on to these negative feelings. After all, he deserves it and more. Forgive me Lord – teach me to forgive.

Forgiveness: undeserved pardon. Was I there to ask Christ's forgiveness as He was crucified for my sins? As His body was tortured and His breath left Him, was I there to say how sorry I was for all my wrong doings? No! Yet, the Lord forgave me before I ever asked!

~ CHAPTER FIVE ~

Was I so righteous and good that I didn't need to be pardoned – that I didn't deserve death. Scripture says: ". . . all have sinned and fall short of the glory of God" (Romans 3:23). I deserve death for my sins. Only Christ lived a sinless life – He deserved life. How great is His mercy and grace. How bountiful is His love to have taken my place on that dreadful cross. When I accept God's complete forgiveness for myself, how can I not forgive others?

Forgiveness: undeserved pardon. The vision of the cross leads to understanding the concept of forgiveness. I am crucified with Christ – therefore I no longer live, but Christ lives in me. Christ in me makes it possible for forgiveness to flow from my heart.

Yes, I was hurt. Yes, my anger grew. Yes, he didn't deserve my pardon. But, that is why it is called "forgiveness."

Learning to Forgive

Think about the sacrifice Christ gave of His own life to bear the sins of the world. Think about all the pain and loneliness He must have experienced at that moment. How often we hear and are taught, over and over again, so many great truths from God's Word. But all too often, these thoughts settle in our minds and do not drop down into the depths of our heart. I had suffered so much pain and bitterness in my soul because I *chose* not to forgive.

When there is no way out, let God in.

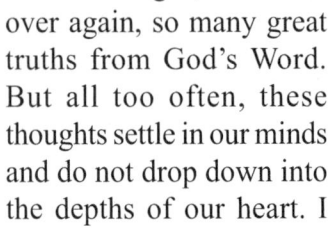

Now that I had begun putting into practice, *choosing* to forgive, I thought I had conquered the holding of grudges.

~ Releasing It to God ~

But then the feelings of unforgiveness would again rear its ugly head in me, and I realized I was still not totally released from the clutches and torment of holding on to this sin of unforgiveness.

Soon, I was again finding myself full of resentment and bitterness. I continually recalled one offense after another. Again, my body began to ache and my mind became depressed. Tears and complaints flowed easily – too easily! To say the words, "I forgive," didn't make the feelings go away. I'd cry out to God, "Help me forgive." I'd say the words and think it was done. But, then later, those old "feelings" would return.

Why was this happening? Because complete understanding had not fully settled into my spirit. The action of *continuing* to forgive had not yet become a common response in my heart. I had to learn to release it to God. I'd say the words, "I forgive," but the knot and the tension were still controlling my body – the offense was still controlling my mind.

God says vengeance is not ours, but His alone:

> *Do not take revenge, my friends, but leave room for God's wrath, for it is written: 'It is mine to avenge; I will repay,' says the Lord. (Romans 12:19)*

I had heard that scripture many times, but I never thought of unforgiveness as a type of vengeance. As far as I could see by the miserable state I was in, unforgiveness was hurting me more than the one I couldn't forgive. What I failed to understand at the time was that by forgiving others, we give God the opportunity to work in their lives.

Getting Even?

As I searched the scriptures on "forgiveness," I found a scripture in the section known as the Lord's prayer which

~ CHAPTER FIVE ~

reads: "Forgive us our debts, as we also have forgiven our debtors" (Matthew 6:12). In this passage, the word "debt" refers to moral debts or sins. When we hold on to unforgiveness, it results in resentment, anger and bitterness in us. We also hold God back from moving in that situation. Proverbs 20:22 says: "Do not say, 'I'll pay you back for this wrong!' Wait for the Lord, and he will deliver you." Yes, God will repay the wicked for their actions.

The writer of Hebrews stresses that vengeance is God's prerogative:

> *For we know him who said, 'It is mine to avenge; I will repay,' and again, 'The Lord will judge his people.' It is a dreadful thing to fall into the hands of the living God. (Hebrews 10:30-31)*

In Romans, Paul tells us: "Do not take revenge, my friends, but leave room for God's wrath. . . (Romans 12:19).

The answer is to let God deal with that person. Why carry that weight on your own shoulders when you don't have to. Forgiving is truly a blessing for you as well, because it releases you from those harmful feelings of bitterness and resentment.

Letting God Keep It

The answer to being able to release it to God really lies in our hearts. The Bible tells us: ". . . For out of the overflow of the heart the mouth speaks" (Matthew 12:34). It boils down to how we are thinking. You need to *decide* not to think about it anymore. If it comes to mind, stop those thoughts by saying out loud: "I have forgiven this. God has taken care

It doesn't take any more time to be positive than it does to be negative.

~ *Releasing It to God* ~

of it for me." When you talk back to those negative thoughts, you'll find it amazing how fast they dissipate when confronted. Then, occupy your mind with something else. Through Paul, God's word tells us to think about good things:

> . . .*whatever is true, whatever is noble, whatever is right, whatever is pure, whatever is lovely, whatever is admirable – if anything is excellent or praiseworthy – think about such things. (Philippians 4:8)*

In my quest to learn to forgive, I asked God to remove my stubborn and hard heart. When I have difficulty with unforgiveness, I pray:

> *Forgive me Lord for not loving ___. Forgive me Lord for hardening my heart against ___. Please remove this hardened heart from me, so I will be freed from unforgiveness and free to love ___ as you do. Thank you Lord for understanding the turmoil within me. Thank you for the peace you are restoring to my soul. Thank you for the gift of Your sacrifice so I may forgive and receive forgiveness. You love ___ and you are in me. Because your love is in me, I am able to love ___ also.*

When I do this, I let Christ's complete sacrifice and total forgiveness for me run deep into my heart, and with it comes a total release from the spirit of unforgiveness. The wonderful "side effect" is an indefinable peace that comes with forgiving.

God has provided for your peace, and He is ready, willing and able to take your pain away. But, it's up to you to release it – it's your choice – *every time* the memories reoccur that cause unforgiveness in your heart to take root. Each and every time those old feelings crop up, take them *immediately* to the

~ CHAPTER FIVE ~

Lord. Don't let the seed of unforgiveness grow. Don't water those negative memories and thoughts. You don't want your life to be filled with weeds of resentment, bitterness, and pain.

Unforgiveness is never worth the effort it takes. Give it over to the Lord instead.

Forgiving – God's Way

How does God forgive? First, He places our sin under the sacrifice and blood of Jesus. Then, He says He "remembers our sins no more." We are told they are as far removed as "the east is from the west." So, we can begin getting rid of our bad feelings by not constantly recalling the offenses of others or dwelling on them. The Bible also tells us to forgive one another quickly before the bitterness has time to take root by never letting "the sun go down while you are still angry." This will also avoid giving "the devil a foothold" in your life (Ephesians 4:26-27).

Of course, forgiving a sin doesn't condone it. It doesn't mean that what another person has done or what you may have done was okay. It is not making what was done all right. Releasing it to God – *giving* it over to Him – allows our Creator to take care of the situation in the best way, even though it may be in ways we can't see with our natural eye. Knowing God is taking care of the infraction – better than you or I ever could is very liberating. Jesus encourages us:

> *Come to me, all you who are weary and burdened, and I will give you rest. Take my yoke upon you and learn from me, for I am gentle and humble in heart, and you will find rest for your souls. For my yoke is easy and my burden is light. (Matthew 11:28-30)*

If we forgive others and ourselves as God has, then we will no longer feel a need to keep bringing the offense up – to keep rehashing it, to keep thinking about it, and to keep anguishing over it. Once we really forgive, the memories won't keep coming back to haunt us over and over again. And, we will be released from the anguish and pain those memories once brought with them.

Kindness Is a Weapon

Paul tells us what we *can* do:

> *Be kind and compassionate to one another, forgiving each other, just as in Christ God forgave you. (Ephesians 4:32)*

Paul encourages us not to "repay anyone evil for evil" and to be "careful to do what is right in the eyes of everybody" (Romans 12:17). In a passage from Proverbs, kindness is encouraged towards your enemy as a means of overcoming evil with good. Paul quotes this same passage:

> *. . . If your enemy is hungry, feed him; if he is thirsty, give him something to drink. In doing this, you will heap burning coals on his head. (Romans 12:20)*

Paul follows that quotation with this statement: "Do not be overcome by evil, but overcome evil with good" (Romans 12:21).

Learning to Love

We are to put the principle of love into action: "Above all, love each other deeply, because love covers over a multitude of sins" (1 Peter 4:8). The Psalmist tells us: ". . . the meek will inherit the land and enjoy great peace" (Psalms 37:11). Looking at the dictionary definition of "meek," we find it

~ CHAPTER FIVE ~

means "enduring injury with patience and without resentment." It also means "submissive" and "humble."

In Galatians, we learn: ". . . if someone is caught in a sin, you who are spiritual should restore him gently. . . ." (Galatians 6:1). And, James tells us how to address this issue and why:

> *My brothers, if one of you should wander from the truth and someone should bring him back, remember this: Whoever turns a sinner from the error of his way will save him from death and cover over a multitude of sins. (James 5:19-20)*

In 2 Corinthians 13:10, Paul states that the authority the Lord gives us is for building others up, not for tearing them down. And, then in Ephesians he concludes:

> *Be completely humble and gentle; be patient, bearing with one another in love. Make every effort to keep the unity of the Spirit through the bond of peace. (Ephesians 4:2-3)*

What do we learn from all this? God wants us to understand the meaning of unconditional love. He wants us all to learn to love as He does. Paul sums it up this way:

> *Therefore, as God's chosen people, holy and dearly loved, clothe yourselves with compassion, kindness, humility, gentleness and patience. Bear with each other and forgive whatever grievances you may have against one another. Forgive as the Lord forgave you. And over all these virtues put on love, which binds them all together in perfect unity. (Colossians 3:12-14)*

~ Releasing It to God ~

*Put on love –
it can be worn
in any kind of weather.*

~ CHAPTER SIX ~

The Past, Present, and Future

Some people worry frantically about the future; others absorb themselves in living in the past; and some concern themselves with both – so much so they can never enjoy the present. I'm one who has been guilty of doing both. What about you? Do you continually worry about the future? Are you preoccupied with the past? Where are you? Do you fluctuate between the two? Are your thoughts filled with so much unproductive and unconstructive worry that you never enjoy a moment's peace? Between worrying about the future and reliving the past in your thoughts, you soon have no time for the present. But, Jesus doesn't want us to live that way.

What Does God Have to Say to Us About This?

> *Therefore I tell you, do not worry about your life, what you will eat or drink; or about your*

~ CHAPTER SIX ~

> *body, what you will wear. Is not life more important than food, and the body more important than clothes?. . .Who of you by worrying can add a single hour to his life? (Matthew 6:25, 27)*

Think about that. Has any of your worrying ever changed anything? Paul advises:

> *Do not be anxious about anything, but in everything, by prayer and petition, with thanksgiving, present your requests to God. (Philippians 4:6)*

This verse tells us not to worry about *anything* – instead pray about *everything*. This includes the big *and* the little things of life. If it's important enough for you to worry about it, it's important enough for you to pray about it. Tell God your needs and then don't forget to thank Him for His answers – even *before* you receive them, because you know your answer is coming. Sometimes you will need to exercise patience because the Lord isn't always on the same time schedule we are hoping Him to be on. David encourages us to: "Wait for the Lord; be strong and take heart and wait for the Lord" (Psalm 27:14). The Psalmist also put patience into practice in his own life: "I wait for the Lord, my soul waits, and in his word I put my hope" (Psalms 130:5).

Jesus died so we wouldn't have to live in the past. Remember what water baptism symbolizes? It is an outward expression of our acceptance of Jesus Christ as our Savior. Being immersed in water symbolizes Christ's death. As a result of His death, we receive forgiveness of our sins. Going under

We were made human beings, not worry warts.

the water symbolizes the death of our old life. Coming up out of the water symbolizes Christ's being raised from the dead. As a result of His resurrection, we receive salvation – eternal life with God. Coming out of the water symbolizes the beginning of a clean, fresh, *new* life:

> *We were therefore buried with him through baptism into death in order that, just as Christ was raised from the dead through the glory of the Father, we too may live a new life.*
> *(Romans 6:4)*

Our identity changes. We become a new person in Christ: "Therefore, if anyone is in Christ, he is a new creation; the old has gone, the new has come" (2 Corinthians 5:17). Christ becomes the center of our life – no matter what happens around us. Did God offer us a problem-free, trouble-free life? No, He didn't. Sure, all of us would like it better if we didn't have so many "problems" in life. But, instead of problems, we should think of them in terms of "challenges." Then, instead of worrying about what might be perceived as unsolvable problems, the focus becomes looking for solutions.

When in Trouble – Pray!

Thankfully, God in His infinite wisdom doesn't leave us without help. Through the guidance of the indwelling Holy Spirit, we are given the wisdom to find the *right* solutions. James offers us the best place to start when these situations arise: "Is any one of you in trouble? He should pray. . . ." (James 5:13). We are encouraged by the Psalmist:

> *The righteous cry out, and the Lord hears them; He delivers them from all their troubles.*
> *(Psalms 34:17)*

~ CHAPTER SIX ~

Notice the Psalm doesn't say the Lord will deliver us from one trouble or a few troubles, but from all our troubles.

Should we pretend we don't have any problems? Of course not. Repressed feelings are not healthy. Imagine blowing up a balloon until it is filled to overflowing. What will eventually happen to that balloon? It will eventually burst! The same thing can happen to us.

If we keep "stuffing" and holding our feelings in for too long, we will eventually explode – either in a fit of anger or through sickness and depression or all of the above. It never helps to repress feelings of hurt and anger. But, it is important to express feelings and emotions in an appropriate manner – first and foremost to God. He is always waiting to listen. He is the one who can deliver us from life's insurmountable problems.

> *Trouble comes, but it doesn't have to overcome.*

God never tells us to repress our feelings; neither do we have to let our emotions control us. Instead, you should "give them away" – not through vented rage at others, but to the Lord. Yes, that's right. God's shoulders are much broader than our own, and He wants us to give Him all our burdens and troubles:

> *'Come to me, all you who are weary and burdened, and I will give you rest. . . . For my yoke is easy and my burden is light.' (Matthew 11:28,30)*

Leaving It With the Lord

That's right – Jesus wants you to "Cast all your anxiety on him . . ." (I Peter 5:7). "Cast" means "to cause to move by throwing" much like using a fishing rod to cast (throw) a

~ *The Past, Present, and Future* ~

fishing lure. "Cast" also means "to throw off or away, to get rid of or to discard." When you discard something, you don't get it back. So, when you have given your problem over to the Lord, leave it there – don't take it back.

To illustrate this, let's say you have a broken watch and you take it to the jeweler to be fixed. He tells you he can fix it, but you need to leave it with him. Do you take the watch back home with you, or do you leave it there with the jeweler? If you want it fixed, you leave it, right? It is the same with your problems. If you want them fixed, you leave them with the Lord.

If you have concerns – financial, personal, business – whatever they may be, turn them over to the Lord. Pray and He will answer. Best of all, He will always do what is best for you. Jesus prayed to the Father: ". . . Yet, not as I will, but as you will" (Matthew 26:39). Completely surrender to the will of God and He will give you the victory.

> *We should run to the throne before we run to the phone.*

Keep in mind that while it's sometimes helpful to analyze our past to work out issues, we have to live in the present. Sometimes the past remains with us too much. What has gone before is just that – gone. We can't relive the past but we can do the best we can right now. Every day is a new opportunity, not to change the past, but to make a new today. And, even though the future is still ahead, we can't get caught up in worrying about it, because we don't know what the future holds:

> *Therefore do not worry about tomorrow, for tomorrow will worry about itself. Each day has enough trouble of its own. (Matthew 6:34)*

As Jesus says, just take care of this day and all its troubles. There is no need to worry about tomorrow until it gets here.

~ CHAPTER SIX ~

God Is For You

There is an account in the Old Testament of a servant of the Lord who was given a word from God for a particular king. This king was about to go into battle against a mighty army. That vast army coming against God's people can also be representative of the problems you may be facing. Listen to what the Lord says:

> ... *'Do not be afraid or discouraged because of this vast army [many problems]. For the battle is not yours, but God's...You will not have to fight this battle. Take up your positions; stand firm and see the deliverance the Lord will give you... Do not be afraid; do not be discouraged. Go out to face them tomorrow, and the Lord will be with you.' (2 Chronicles 20:15,17, Comments in brackets added)*

Yes, we have to face our problems, but always remember – *God will be with us.* Sometimes He will deliver us from our problems, but other times He will stand with us as we go through and deal with those problems. Do not be afraid and do not be discouraged. Paul tells us: "... If God is for us, who can be against us?" (Romans 8:31) and "... in all things we are more than conquerors through him who loved us" (Romans 8:37). When we stop living in the past and stop worrying about the future, we are freed to live in the present.

God Is Always There

In the book of Exodus, God told Moses to go back to Egypt in order to confront Pharaoh and bring the Israelites out of Egypt. At this point in history, the Israelites had been slaves in Egypt for four centuries. Still, they continued to worship

~ *The Past, Present, and Future* ~

the one true God, the Creator and Ruler of the universe – the One perfect in power, wisdom and goodness.

On the other hand, the Egyptians worshipped literally hundreds of various types of people, objects, images, and practically *anything* in nature as "gods" – on earth or in the sky. For example, they had many local gods up and down the land, a state god, household and lesser gods, including a god of learning and the moon, a war-god and a god that overshadowed the war-god, a goddess of joy, and a god of vegetation. Plus, they had cosmic gods: the sun-god, the god of truth, justice and cosmic order, the sky-goddess, as well as the gods of air, earth and waters.

This was quite a contrast from our self-sufficient Creator. Is it any wonder that Moses did not know what name to give the Lord? In Exodus we read:

> *Moses said to God, 'Suppose I go to the Israelites and say to them, The God of your fathers has sent me to you, and they ask me, What is his name? Then what shall I tell them?' God said to Moses, 'I AM WHO I AM. This is what you are to say to the Israelites: I AM has sent me to you.' (Exodus 3:13-14)*

In this scripture, God calls Himself: "I AM WHO I AM." This name expressed His characteristics of dependability, faithfulness, and eternal stability. God desired the full trust of His people. Notice, He did not refer to Himself as "I WAS" or "I WILL BE." The name, "I AM" is in the present tense. He is God of the present.

Oh yes! God is ever-*present* in your life. He wants to bless you *now*. He loves you *now*. He cares about us not just collectively as His church, but also each of us individually. Our Heavenly Father cares about what is going on in your life *now*. We know that because Peter tells us: "Cast all your anxiety on him because he cares for you" (I Peter 5:7).

~ CHAPTER SIX ~

God even cares about what you may consider the smallest things. I'm reminded of an incident in my life that caused me to understand this fully. One evening after a long day at work, and a stop at the store on the way home, I was overwhelmed with fatigue. As I pulled into the parking lot of my apartment complex, I watched as another car pulled into the last open parking space near the sidewalk that led back to my home.

I then pulled into a space on the far side of the parking lot. Feeling completely drained of all energy, I sat there wondering how I was going to make it to the house. As I told the Lord how I was feeling, I also noticed no one had gotten out of the other car. Just then, it began to pull back out. I thought, "Oh, they must have the wrong building," because visitors did tend to get lost when first coming into this huge complex. I quickly took advantage of my new found opportunity to save a few steps and pulled around to the closer parking space.

To my surprise, the mysterious car parked further up, but the occupants walked down to the end of the same building I was in. The only reason they moved their car that would seem reasonable to me was that God prompted them to do so. They had originally parked exactly where they needed to be. In that instance, God showed me how He cares about everything that goes on in our lives – even the most insignificant things. He wanted me to know that and showed me, by saving me from walking that extra distance when I was so overwhelmed with tiredness. I thanked Him as my heart was revived with joy at knowing that He does care – even about the smallest details of our lives.

So, why try to handle and work out all your problems by yourself, when you have a loving and caring Heavenly Father who wants to be a part of your life and wants to help you – even with the smallest things? The past is over, the future hasn't arrived, and today is a new day.

Just realizing how much God cares is enough to fill you with joy. Go for the victory and live in the present where the great "I AM" resides!

~ *The Past, Present, and Future* ~

You laid your eternity in His hands, so put today in His hands, too.

~ CHAPTER SEVEN ~

What About Fears?

What about fears? We all grow up with one kind of fear or another. Quite a few of us have more than one. Sometimes we hold on to fears leftover from childhood. Sometimes they are instilled in us from the "bad news" on television and on the radio or from what we read in the newspapers and magazines. Sometimes, the bad experiences we've had in our lives leave us full of fears. Sometimes, people even find themselves living in a continual state of fear. Peace and lack of fear shouldn't be an occasional blessing but should become commonplace in our lives.

A Helpful Study

To do a "word study" in the Bible on this subject use a Concordance or a book on Bible topics and look up the word "fear" and other related words. Examples of words that relate to fear could be: afraid, worry, anxiety, hope, trust, faith, stress, peace, apprehension, doubt, unbelief, faithfulness, and confidence. All these references will help you to have God's perspective on this subject. Doing a study like this is helpful when overwhelmed by any type of problem.

Love Conquers Fear

Fear of any kind can be overwhelming at times. It is helpful to find friends who will pray for you and with you. James tells us: ". . . The prayer of a righteous man is powerful and effective" (James 5:16).

In John we read: "God is love. . .There is no fear in love. But perfect love drives out fear" (I John 4:16, 18). And in Isaiah, God lovingly reminds us:

> *So do not fear, for I am with you; do not be dismayed, for I am your God. I will strengthen you and help you; I will uphold you with my righteous right hand. (Isaiah 41:10)*

Faith Replaces Fear

Simply put, fear is "wrong believing," a negative reaction that can literally attract what we fear the most. Job expressed it this way: "What I feared has come upon me; what I dreaded has happened to me" (Job 3:25). To overcome fear, we must replace it with "faith" which is the direct opposite. Faith attracts to you what you do want. Even more, where faith is, fear cannot exist. Therefore, the more faith, the less fear you will have until eventually you will no longer fear that particular problem.

God encourages us to let go of fear by trusting in Him. David was rejoicing as he said:

~ What About Fears? ~

The Lord is my light and my salvation – whom shall I fear? The Lord is the stronghold of my life – of whom shall I be afraid? (Psalms 27:1)

God Himself declares in Isaiah:

For I am the Lord, your God, who takes hold of your right hand and says to you, Do not fear; I will help you. (Isaiah 41:13)

David shows us what we can expect by seeking and depending on the Lord: "I sought the Lord, and he answered me; he delivered me from all my fears" (Psalms 34:4).

Fear does not come from God – He doesn't want us living in fear. If you are, then cast it out in the name of Jesus this very moment. Begin today replacing fear with faith and let God's love surround you. Jesus said: "Peace I leave with you; my peace I give you. . . Do not let your hearts be troubled and do not be afraid" (John 14:27). We have a choice to make. Don't choose to live by fear, but rather choose to live by faith. Step out today and take a leap of faith, and God will reward you greatly by removing those feelings of fear from your life.

If God said it, that settles it!

Fearing God

The Bible is the Word of God. It is a book of *promises and blessings.* It is also the *book of life.* It is a beautiful *love letter* to us from our Heavenly Father. It is a book about the past, about today, and about the future. It is the story of God's people, a story that presents to us the very heart and character of God.

~ CHAPTER SEVEN ~

There is passage after passage in the Bible that says, "Fear not!" or "Do not be afraid." But there is also passage after passage that says, "Fear God." Is there a contradiction here? Are we supposed to be afraid of God? What does "Fear God" mean?

First let's review some things we shouldn't fear. The Psalmist says: "I will fear no evil, for you are with me; . . ." (Psalms 23:4) and ". . . The Lord is the stronghold of my life – of whom shall I be afraid?" (Psalms 27:1).

In contrast, David tells us: "Fear the Lord, you his saints, for those who fear him lack nothing" (Psalms 34:9). Samuel tells the people: ". . .be sure to fear the Lord and serve him faithfully with all your heart; consider what great things he has done for you" (I Samuel 12:24). The Psalmist proclaims: "Let all the earth fear the Lord; Let all the people of the world revere him" (Psalms 33:8).

What does the "fear of Lord" mean? Are we talking about the terror of "fire and brimstone" judgment? Are we to be frightened of God because He is so powerful and we are so lowly compared to Him?

Looking up the word "fear" in Scripture, I found that it is represented by three different words in Hebrew and one word in Greek. The original meaning in the ancient languages was often closer to "reverent" or "reverence" – to revere or to hold in awe and to be afraid of that awesomeness.

Looking up "fear" in the dictionary, I found one of the definitions was "to have a reverential awe of." The example that was given was to "fear God." The meaning of "revere" is to fear out of respect or "to show devoted honor to." Other words with similar meanings are to "worship," "adore," and "venerate" – "to venerate" means "holding as holy because of character, association, or age."

~ What About Fears? ~

The Example of Job

> *In the land of Uz there lived a man whose name was Job. This man was blameless and upright; he feared God and shunned evil. (Job 1:1)*

Job was a man that was spiritually and morally upright. Because of his "fear of God," his respect for and devotion to the Lord, Job deliberately avoided anything with the appearance of evil.

Our life here on earth is a continual growing process. It is one big classroom. But, Christ is our measuring stick – not each other. We want to *glorify* God in all we do and say. We want it said of us that we were "blameless and upright" as it was said of Job. We want God to be able to say: "Well done, good and faithful servant! . . ." (Matthew 25:21). And, Paul encourages us to: ". . . Aim for perfection. . ." (2 Corinthians 13:11).

There may be times when we don't always do what we should. But, we serve a Lord that will continually forgive us if we ask Him. He says He will take those sins and remember them no more. When He looks at us, He sees us clothed in the righteousness of Christ.

Job tells us: ". . . The fear of the Lord – that is wisdom, and to shun evil is understanding" (Job 28:28). The Psalmist puts it this way: "The fear of the Lord is the beginning of wisdom; all who follow his precepts have good understanding" (Psalms 111:10). To follow His precepts means to do them. And Solomon wrote: "The fear of the Lord is the beginning of wisdom, and knowledge of the Holy One is understanding" (Proverbs 9:10).

Other verses that describe "the fear of the Lord" are:

> *To fear the Lord is to hate evil. . . (Proverbs 8:13)*

~ CHAPTER SEVEN ~

The fear of the Lord is the beginning of knowledge. . . (Proverbs 1:7)

A wise man fears the Lord and shuns evil. . . (Proverbs 14:16)

Blessed is the man who fears the Lord, who finds great delight in his commands. (Psalms 112:1)

Keeping His Commandments

How did David feel about God's law, His commands, and His general principles for living? Here is his answer:

Oh, how I love your law! I meditate on it all day long. Your commands make me wiser than my enemie. . . I have more insight than all my teachers, for I meditate on your statutes. I have more understanding than the elders, for I obey your precepts. I have kept my feet from every evil path so that I might obey your word. (Psalms 119:97-101)

Now I want to go back to the time of Israel in the Old Testament when Moses said to the people:

. . . what does the Lord your God ask of you but to fear the Lord your God, to walk in all his ways, to love him, to serve the Lord your God with all your heart and with all your soul, and to observe the Lord's commands and decrees that I am giving you today for your own good? (Deuteronomy. 10:12-13)

~ What About Fears? ~

How do we fear Him? – by walking in His ways, by loving Him, by serving Him, by obedience to His commands. Why? "For your own good." Moses also said:

> The Lord commanded us to obey all these decrees and to fear the Lord our God, so that we might always prosper and be kept alive . . . (Deuteronomy. 6:24)

For those of you who are parents, do you have rules for your children to follow? Why? Do you set these rules because you don't like your children and because you want to make life miserable for them or because you just want to give them a hard time? I don't think so. It is because you love them. You want what is best for them, and you want to protect them. So, you set parameters for them – you lay out rules for them to obey. For example, you tell them: "Don't run out into the street; don't accept rides from strangers; don't stay out late, etc."

How many of you questioned your parents' commands or rules? For instance, "Why can't I stay out after 10 PM like all the other kids?" The reply probably was: "It's for your own good" – just like the Lord tells us in Deuteronomy 10:13. I wonder how many parents knew they were quoting scripture when they said that?

God's commandments teach us how to love Him and how to love others. Paul tells us to:

> Let no debt remain outstanding, except the continuing debt to love one another, for he who loves his fellow man has fulfilled the law. . . . Love does no harm to its neighbor. Therefore love is the fulfillment of the law. (Romans 13:8, 10)

~ CHAPTER SEVEN ~

John writes:

> *This is love for God: to obey his commands. And his commands are not burdensome, for everyone born of God overcomes the world. (I John 5:3-4)*

Christ summed them up in this statement and it is exactly what He did for each one of us:

> *My command is this: Love each other as I have loved you. Greater love has no one than this, that he lay down his life for his friends. (John 15:12-13)*

Coming Judgment

But what about the fire and brimstone teachings that portray a harsh, untouchable God? Jesus tells us:

> *Do not be afraid of those who kill the body but cannot kill the soul. Rather, be afraid of the One who can destroy both soul and body in hell. (Matthew 10:28)*

The first part of that verse is speaking about men – the second part about God. It is God alone who determines our final destiny. Paul tells us:

> *For we must all appear before the judgment seat of Christ, that each one may receive what is due him for the things done while in the body, whether good or bad. (2 Corinthians 5:10)*

David tells us: "The Lord watches over all who love him, but all the wicked he will destroy" (Psalms 145:20). In this respect, "to fear him" as in the definition of being afraid is very appropriate because Jesus Christ is the One to whom we will be accountable on Judgment Day. But, since we have accepted Christ as our Savior, we have nothing to fear in the Lord! With joy and thanksgiving we can praise the Lord for His goodness and love.

From the Psalms, we find instruction in "the fear of the Lord:"

> *Come, my children, listen to me; I will teach you the fear of the Lord. Whoever of you loves life and desires to see many good days, keep your tongue from evil and your lips from speaking lies. Turn from evil and do good; seek peace and pursue it. (Psalms 34:11-14)*

Again, in this passage, fear or reverence for the Lord is described as a way of speaking and acting. It is turning from following a way that brings destruction to following a way that brings goodness and life.

There are many benefits to "fearing the Lord" – in loving, trusting and obeying Him. Those who do are called blessed: "Blessed are all who fear the Lord, who walk in his ways" (Psalms 128:1).

Our Way – Or God's Way

In Isaiah the Lord declared: ". . . neither are your ways my ways. . . As the heavens are higher than the earth, so are my ways higher than your ways . . ." (Isaiah 55:8-9). How can we describe the perfect ways of God? The Bible gives us a multitude of Scriptures that tell us how His ways are perfect, just, loving, faithful, holy, and righteous. Here are just a few examples:

> *As for God, his way is perfect. . . (2 Samuel 22:31)*

~ CHAPTER SEVEN ~

> *... and all his ways are just... (Deuteronomy. 32:4)*

> *All the ways of the Lord are loving and faithful for those who keep the demands of his covenant. (Psalms 25:10)*

> *Your ways, O God, are holy... (Psalms 77:13)*

> *The Lord is righteous in all his ways... (Psalms 145:17)*

In contrast, we are also told:

> *There is a way that seems right to a man, but in the end it leads to death." (Proverbs 16:25)*

> *All a man's ways seem innocent to him, but motives are weighed by the Lord. (Proverbs 16:2).*

Taking a look at some examples of God putting "His ways" into practice, we find the Lord:

> *... is gracious and compassionate, slow to anger and rich in love. (Psalms 145:8)*

> *... is good to all; he has compassion on all he has made. (Psalms 145:9)*

> *... is faithful to all his promises and loving toward all he has made. (Psalms 145:13)*

> *... upholds all those who fall and lifts up all who are bowed down. (Psalms 145:14)*

~ *What About Fears?* ~

. . . is near to all who call on him, to all who call on him in truth. (Psalms 145:18)

. . . fulfills the desires of those who fear him; he hears their cry and saves them. (Psalms 145:19)

. . . watches over all who love him, but all the wicked he will destroy. (Psalms 145:20)

. . . upholds the cause of the oppressed and gives food to the hungry. (Psalms 146:7)

. . . sets prisoners free. . . gives sight to the blind. . . lifts up those who are bowed down. . . loves the righteous. (Psalms 146:8)

. . . sustains the fatherless and the widow, but he frustrates the ways of the wicked. (Psalm 146:9)

. . . heals the brokenhearted and binds up their wounds. (Psalms 147:3)

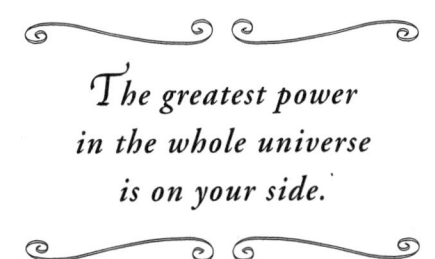

*The greatest power
in the whole universe
is on your side.*

From Proverbs we learn:

. . . the Lord gives wisdom, and from his mouth come knowledge and understanding. He holds

~ CHAPTER SEVEN ~

> *victory in store for the upright, he is a shield to those whose walk is blameless, for he guards the course of the just and protects the way of his faithful ones. (Proverbs 2:6-8)*

Why then should you trust and obey Him? Because He Loves You! Because He wants to take care of you! Because He wants every good thing for you!

Benefits and Rewards

Now that we've covered some of "the ways" of God and His character, let's cover the benefits or rewards of "fearing the Lord." We have seen that fearing Him is the same as obeying Him, loving Him, trusting Him, honoring Him, and worshiping Him. God has promised to give those who fear Him: salvation, mercy, love, righteousness, provision, help, blessings, His presence, wealth, honor, and life:

> *Surely his salvation is near those who fear him, that his glory may dwell in our land. (Psalms 85:9)*

> *. . .he does not treat us as our sins deserve or repay us according to our iniquities. (Psalms 103:10)*

> *He provides food [provision for daily needs] for those who fear him; he remembers his covenant forever. (Psalms 111:5, comments in brackets added)*

> *You who fear him, trust in the Lord – he is their help and shield. (Psalms 115:11)*

~ What About Fears? ~

He will bless those who fear the Lord – small and great alike. (Psalms 115:13)

Let those who fear the Lord say: 'His love endures forever.' (Psalms 118:4)

The Lord is with me; He is my helper. (Psalms 118:7)

Humility and the fear of the Lord bring wealth and honor and life. (Proverbs 22:4)

The ultimate result of "fearing the Lord" is that you will delight God and bring Him pleasure. The Psalmist tells us: "the Lord delights in those who fear him, who put their hope in his unfailing love" (Psalms 147:11). Make it your goal to follow God's example by following His ways. His character is illustrated in His commandments which show us how to love – for God is love. May you "walk in the fear of God" by walking in love and honoring His name!

~ CHAPTER EIGHT ~

Eternal Life

*D*o you *think* you know God or do you truly know Him? Through the Bible – His Word – He reveals His character, His ways, and His plans. God's love for us is real and He has so much to give us. Jesus said: "If you really knew me, you would know my Father as well...Anyone who has seen me has seen the Father..." (John 14:7,9). He said this because the words He spoke and the miracles He did represented the works of the Father.

The "Word of God" tells us that Jesus is the only way to eternal life. Jesus told His disciple Thomas, "I am the way and the truth and the life. No one comes to the Father except through me" (John 14:6). Speaking about Jesus, Peter said to the people:

~ CHAPTER EIGHT ~

> *Salvation is found in no one else, for there is no other name under heaven given to men by which we must be saved. (Acts 4:12)*

When Paul and Silas were asked what to do in order to be saved, they replied: ". . . 'Believe in the Lord Jesus, and you will be saved – you and your household' (Acts 16:31). Paul added:

> *. . .if you confess with your mouth, 'Jesus is Lord,' and believe in your heart that God raised him from the dead, you will be saved. (Romans 10:9-10)*

Peter replied to the question, "what shall we do?" by saying:

> *. . . Repent and be baptized, every one of you, in the name of Jesus Christ for the forgiveness of your sins. And you will receive the gift of the Holy Spirit. (Acts 2:38)*

When we believe in Christ as our Savior, the Holy Spirit is also imparted to us, witnessing to our spirit that we now have eternal life:

> *And you also were included in Christ when you heard the word of truth, the gospel of your salvation. Having believed, you were marked in him with a seal, the promised Holy Spirit, who is a deposit guaranteeing our inheritance. . . (Ephesians 1:13-14)*

The Bible tells us that:

> Through the sacrificial death of Jesus, our sins are forgiven. (See Romans 4:25)

~ Eternal Life ~

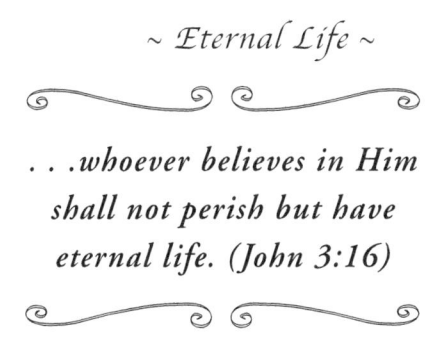

...whoever believes in Him shall not perish but have eternal life. (John 3:16)

By the resurrection of Jesus, we receive the gift of eternal life. (See Romans 6:22)

After His resurrection, Jesus ascended to Heaven to sit at the right hand of God the Father in Heaven. (See Ephesians 1:20)

The Holy Spirit was then sent and made available to us. (See John 16:7)

By the spilling of Christ's blood the veil or the curtain that separated us from the Father because of our sins was torn, which now allows us to go directly to God the Father in prayer. (See Luke 23:44-46, Hebrews 9:12, 24, 10:19-22)

We become God's children when we except Jesus as Lord and Savior. (See John 1:12)

It doesn't matter how good you are, how many things you did right – somewhere in your life, you committed a sin. We are told the wages of sin is death. You only have to commit *one* sin to be guilty of them all – they all receive the same penalty, the end result is the same. One sin is so offensive to God – so against His nature – that it cancels out and overrides all the good you have done or could ever do.

~ CHAPTER EIGHT ~

So we can't earn salvation, because we just don't have in us what it takes to live a sinless life.

Even if you could somehow get through life without sinning, you still could not get into heaven. Why? Because the Bible tells us that all men are born sinners:

> *Therefore, just as sin entered the world through one man, and death through sin, and in this way death came to all men, because all sinned...*
> *(Romans 5:12)*

In other words, all of us are born with the "stain" of sin in our lives from day one. Even if you could – theoretically – lead a "sinless" life, you would still be guilty and undeserving of salvation. You've lost the opportunity for eternal life in His kingdom by default.

Are you beginning to understand why you can't work your way into the kingdom of heaven? Because of sin – the violation of God's law, which represents His character and His love for creation – you've been automatically disqualified.

Now what about the One who did live a sinless, righteous life in every way and did qualify to receive eternal life. Now, if you or I could have done that we possibly could have saved our own life but no one else's. How is it when Christ paid the penalty, which is death, He saved all of us, you and me, and everyone down through the generations who would accept Him as their Savior. The answer lies in the fact that His life was worth more than all of us put together. His life was worth more than all of mankind.

How can this be you ask? Think of the Bible as a treasure map leading the way to the treasure. Jesus Christ will be the treasure because it is through Him that we receive eternal life in the presence of a loving God, with joys unspeakable for evermore. Now when you follow a treasure map, it takes you from place to place, picking up clues along the way until you reach your destination – the treasure.

~ Eternal Life ~

The Priceless Gift of Christ's Life

The first spot on our treasure map is Genesis: "In the beginning God created the heavens and the earth" (Genesis 1:1). In Hebrew the word translated "God" is "Elohiym" which is a plural noun. Familiar words that we use in our language today that are considered plural nouns are such words as church, sheep, and family. They are each a singular word, but they mean more than one member. Now let's go on in Genesis: "Then God said, 'Let us make man in our image, in our likeness, . . . (Genesis 1:26). Here again we see the use of the words "us" and "our" indicating God is plural.

Following our map we move on to the book of John:

> *In the beginning was the Word, and the Word was with God, and the Word was God. He was with God in the beginning. Through him all things were made; without him nothing was made that has been made. (John 1:1-3)*

> *The Word became flesh and made his dwelling among us. We have seen his glory, the glory of the One and Only, who came from the Father, full of grace and truth. (John 1:14)*

> *For the law was given through Moses; grace and truth came through Jesus Christ. No one has ever seen God, but God the One and Only, who is at the Father's side, has made him known. (John 1:17-18)*

> *...regarding his Son... who through the Spirit of holiness was declared with power to be the Son of God by his resurrection from the dead: Jesus Christ our Lord. (Romans 1:3,4)*

~ CHAPTER EIGHT ~

These verses make it very clear that Jesus was originally a member of the Godhead. We have found our true treasure. But, just to confirm this, follow our map to Hebrews:

> ... he has spoken to us by his Son, whom he appointed heir of all things, and through whom he made the universe. . . . But about the Son he says, 'Your throne, O God, will last for ever and ever, and righteousness will be the scepter of your kingdom. (Hebrews 1:2,8)

Now, let's follow our treasure map and see that Jesus was also truly human. Mary was the chosen mother of Jesus. She was a virgin and engaged to a man named Joseph. Both Mary and Joseph were descendents of David. When Mary conceived, an angel of God came to her saying:

> "Greetings, you who are highly favored! The Lord is with you. . .Do not be afraid, Mary, you have found favor with God. (Luke 1:28, 30)

The angel continued speaking to her about the conception of Jesus coming from the impregnation by the Holy Spirit (See Luke 1:26-35). Concerning the future of her son, Jesus, the angel said: "He will be great and will be called the Son of the Most High. . ." (Luke 1:32)

The fact that Jesus Christ was born of a woman shows us that even though His origins were divine, He had emptied Himself of that position to become human:

> But when the time had fully come, God sent his Son, born of a woman, born under law, to redeem those under law. . . (Galatians 4:4)

> The Word became flesh and made his dwelling among us. . . (John 1:14)

~ Eternal Life ~

> . . .regarding his Son, who as to his human nature was a descendant of David. . .
> (Romans 1:3)

Because Christ's life, as a member of the Godhead, was worth more than all of humanity, and because He lived a perfect life, without sin, as a human man, He could step in and pay the penalty for your sin. You no longer have to pay this penalty yourself. You have been pardoned. The price has been paid. The prison door has been opened. You are freed.

God's Awesome Love

Can you begin to comprehend, even a little bit, how awesome and great God's love is for you. He looked down upon you and saw all your sins, all your wrong doings, yet He had mercy on you – compassion for you flowed from His heart. Despite the things you did, He still loved you. You broke His heart, and you kindled His anger against you when you went down the wrong path, but still, He continued to care about you.

What you deserved and what you received were two very different things. He showed you mercy and gave you grace and forgiveness. Why? Because of "His great love for [you]" (Ephesians 2:4). No, you didn't get what you deserved – how great His love was towards you!

Even though you were busy doing your own thing, whether it pleased God or not, whether it hurt yourself or someone else, being oblivious to God's love and plan for you, He let His son take your place in the court room and stand in epoxy for you and went as far as to take His life, in your place.

Certainly, you can now see how grace enters into saving you. If it wasn't for grace – His love, His unmerited favor, and His exceptional kindness, He would never have bothered to send His Son in the first place, to make your salvation possible.

~ CHAPTER EIGHT ~

Believing for Salvation

Does salvation fall into our laps. Are we all automatically saved? We have seen salvation is not by works because it is simply impossible for us to ever be good enough. And, doing the right thing from now on will not pay the penalty for the sins we already committed. But, there is a requirement to be fulfilled by us, in order for the blood He shed to be applied to us. After we receive the knowledge to know we can be saved, we have to have faith – we have to believe in Christ as our Lord and Savior. As Lord, we are saying we accept Him as our master, head, leader who we will now follow. As Savior, we are saying we accept His sacrifice of paying the penalty for us and will receive forgiveness for our sins.

Let's try to simplify this by picturing a guilty person – any one of us – standing in the court room before the judge. All the testimonies for and against you are in, the verdict of guilty is about to be pronounced. But, the judge takes pity on you because of his kindness and extends mercy towards you and offers you the chance to bring forth one more witness for your defense. Because of his grace – his favor – he has given you one more opportunity to be redeemed.

You are excited, full of hope, believing – knowing there is one more person you can bring in to defend you. You just know this person will be able to save you from the guilty verdict that is about to be pronounced on your life. For us, that person is Jesus, He is our defense:

> *... if anybody does sin, we have one who speaks to the Father in our defense – Jesus Christ, the Righteous One. He is the atoning sacrifice for our sins, and not only for ours but also for the sins of the whole world. (I John 2:1-2)*

Here in lies our requirement – our faith in believing Jesus is our defense. When we believe He can save us because He took our place and paid the price of death for our wrong deeds – He comes to our defense and the judge pronounces the verdict – not guilty. When you except Christ, you will receive eternal life. Jesus said: "I give them eternal life, and they shall never perish. . ." (John 10:28).

Believing is a choice you make. God doesn't force anything on you. He has given you free will, but He wants you to choose life. Why, because He loves you and wants to fellowship with you forever. If you don't believe, that is your choice. But, you also won't receive eternal life with Him, just because He paid the penalty for you. Faith is required to receive this gift, this promise of salvation.

Here is an analogy to help simplify it. The postman comes to your door with a package for you. He has brought you a gift from a friend. You didn't order it or ask for it. You didn't work for it, so you didn't earn it. It's a gift because it is being given to you. Someone cares a great deal about you. It is out of their love for you that you are being given this gift. But, it was sent by certified mail which means you need to sign for it before it can be given to you. The postman can't sign your name for you. You need to show your signature in order to receive the gift from the postman. In the same way, you need to show your faith in order to receive salvation.

It's Your Choice

Are you His child? Are you in a position to receive His promises and blessings? Are you beginning to understand how much He loves you. If you haven't believed in the Lord Jesus for salvation before, then – now is the time to pray to God and accept Christ as your personal Lord and Savior. Now is the time to repent of your sins and receive forgiveness. Now is the time to believe in your heart that God raised Jesus Christ from the dead and inherit eternal life with Him.

Better still, you don't have to "work" to receive what has been given to you as a free gift. God loves you and accepts

~ CHAPTER EIGHT ~

you unconditionally – without reservation – just the way you are right here – right now – at this moment in time. You don't have to clean up your act or even put on a "new suit" to receive that gift. After you accept Him by faith, then He will guide and direct your path through the indwelling Holy Spirit and will change your life forever.

You and God make a majority.

~ CHAPTER NINE ~

Starting Over

Did you ever wish you could start your life over? When you accepted Christ as Lord of your life, it was in effect what you were doing. It was the beginning of a new way of living and thinking as you began to follow the example Jesus left you. It was an opportunity to put behind you those things that you felt guilty about, or were ashamed of, or were hurt by, or felt angry and bitter over. Now, you no longer need to feel as though you have to get back at anyone or prove yourself to anyone. It is also an opportunity to learn to walk with a new compassion in your heart towards others:

> *You, my brothers, were called to be free. But do not use your freedom to indulge the sinful nature; rather, serve one another in love. (Galatians 5:13)*

~ CHAPTER NINE ~

Yes, Jesus is giving you that chance to start your life over. As you went through the ritual of baptism, it symbolized your burial and resurrection with Christ – the burial of your "old self," and your rebirth as a "new" person in Christ:

> *. . . don't you know that all of us who were baptized into Christ Jesus were baptized into his death? We were therefore buried with him through baptism into death in order that, just as Christ was raised from the dead through the glory of the Father, we too may live a new life. (Romans 6:3-4)*

Baptism is only a beginning step in a life long process, as you become a new person. In this process, we begin to think and act differently then we ever did before. Rather than following the way that may come naturally to us – which may have seemed right to our "old" selves, we make a definite choice to change the direction of our lives. We begin to follow the example Jesus gave us through the life He lived. Regarding this transformation, we arc told by Paul:

> *Do not conform any longer to the pattern of this world, but be transformed by the renewing of your mind. . .(Romans 12:2)*

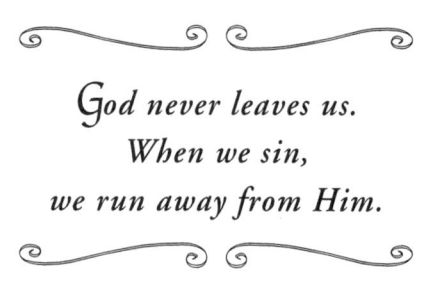

*God never leaves us.
When we sin,
we run away from Him.*

~ Starting Over ~

Our Thought Patterns

Paul takes the "renewing of our minds" a step further by saying, ". . . we take captive every thought to make it obedient to Christ" (2 Corinthians 10:5). In other words, don't just allow thoughts to exist in your mind. You do have the ability to control them. The more you study the word of God, the more you are able to overcome your own negative thoughts and line them up with His word. When necessary, speak "out loud" to stop the thoughts in your mind that you need to take control over.

Since we know that all of our actions and spoken words are preceded by thoughts, we have to have the victory in our minds in order to begin to overcome the fears and problems of this world. As our minds are renewed, we become more "Christ-minded." We do this by filling up daily with the Word of God and allowing the Holy Spirit to work in us and through us. Paul adds:

> *. . .whatever is true, whatever is noble, whatever is right, whatever is pure, whatever is lovely, whatever is admirable – if anything is excellent or praiseworthy – think about such things. (Philippians 4:8)*

And in Ephesians, he tells us:

> *You were taught, with regard to your former way of life, to put off your old self, which is being corrupted by its deceitful desires; to be made new in the attitude of your minds; and to put on the new self, created to be like God in true righteousness and holiness. (Ephesians 4:22-24)*

~ CHAPTER NINE ~

To "put off your old self" involves changing your former way of life to a new way of life. You begin to "put on the new self" by thinking in a new way. But it is only through the grace and salvation of Jesus Christ that we can start over and begin this process of change.

> *When you are going in the wrong direction, God allows U-turns.*

God tells us in Isaiah that: ". . . my thoughts are not your thoughts, neither are your ways my ways. . ." (Isaiah 55:8). But, now we are on our way to lining up our thoughts up with God's thoughts and lining up our ways with His ways. Take note that ". . . God did not call us to be impure, but to live a holy life" (1 Thessalonians 4:7).

Mary's Example

Mary was the chosen mother of Jesus. An angel of God had come to her saying:

> *Greetings, you who are highly favored! The Lord is with you. . . . Do not be afraid, Mary, you have found favor with God. (Luke 1:28, 30)*

Why would God have favored her? What was her heart towards God? We can know these answers by the reply she gave the angel. After he finished instructing her in the will of God for her life, she answered: " 'I am the Lord's servant'. . . 'May it be to me as you have said'. . . (Luke 1:38). Here we see the example of a godly woman who submitted to the Word of God. She was willing to be obedient to whatever He required of her.

Mary's relative, Elizabeth, being led by the Holy Spirit, said of Mary: "Blessed is she who has believed that what the Lord has said to her will be accomplished!" (Luke 1:45). Yes, Mary was a woman full of faith in the Word of God. She believed that whatever God said He would do, that He could and would, bring His word to pass.

Her attributes don't stop here, she also was a praiser – a woman that praised God:

> *And Mary said: 'My soul glorifies the Lord and my spirit rejoices in God my Savior. . . for the Mighty One has done great things for me – holy is his name. (Luke 1:46-47, 49)*

It would have been an awesome blessing to be called to be the mother of Jesus. But, it also would have been a tremendous responsibility to raise the Son of God. Even more than being Jesus' mother, Jesus Himself tells us that it is more blessed to be obedient to God:

> *. . . a woman in the crowd called out, 'Blessed is the mother who gave you birth and nursed you.' He [Jesus] replied, 'Blessed rather are those who hear the word of God and obey it.' (Luke 11:27-28, Comments in brackets added)*

You Have a Helper

After Jesus had been resurrected, it was to be another forty days until He would actually ascend to be with His Father in Heaven. During this time over 500 people were witnesses to His resurrection and had received many convincing proofs that He was alive. He continued to walk with and instruct the apostles and His disciples, speaking to them about the kingdom of God. On one of these occasions, He gave them this command:

> *. . . Do not leave Jerusalem, but wait for the gift my Father promised, which you have heard*

~ CHAPTER NINE ~

*me speak about. For John baptized with water,
but in a few days you will be baptized with the
Holy Spirit. (Acts 1:4-5)*

Shortly after this instruction, His disciples saw Him being taken up before their very eyes until a cloud hid Him from their view. As Jesus ascended towards Heaven, two men perceived to be angels appeared suddenly and said:

*. . .This same Jesus, who has been taken from
you into heaven, will come back in the same way
you have seen him go into heaven.' (Acts 1:11)*

Then, they returned to Jerusalem where they waited together for the coming Holy Spirit. In Acts 1:13-15 you'll find a list of the people who waited for this event to occur. Mary, the mother of Jesus, as well as His brothers were among the group – all joining together in continual prayer in anticipation of what was to come. Then on the day of Pentecost, the Holy Spirit was introduced with the sound of blowing wind and what appeared to be tongues of fire resting on each of them. The scripture continues:

*All of them were filled with the Holy Spirit and
began to speak in other tongues as the Spirit
enabled them. (Acts 2:4)*

After you have accepted Jesus into your heart, the Holy Spirit also comes to dwell in you, to lead and guide you on this new course – to help you do the right things. This is a promise from Jesus Himself:

*. . .the Counselor, the Holy Spirit, whom the
Father will send in my name, will teach you
all things and will remind you of everything I
have said to you." (John 14:26)*

~ Starting Over ~

In Galatians, Paul tells us to "live by the Spirit" so that we won't gratify the desires of the sinful nature. We are then given a list of the virtues that the Holy Spirit produces in us:

> *But the fruit of the Spirit is love, joy, peace, patience, kindness, goodness, faithfulness, gentleness and self-control. . .(Galatians 5:22-23)*

Do you see how much God cares for us? In His goodness, He didn't leave us to struggle on our own. He remains with us, from the moment we accept Him into our heart, "because God has poured out His love into our hearts by the Holy Spirit, whom He has given us" (Romans 5:5). In other words, although at times you may feel weak in a particular area of your life, you will have the ability to conquer the "old you" by controlling your thoughts with the help of the indwelling Holy Spirit. To emphasize how you are able to stop doing those things that are harmful to you or others and displeasing to God – it is "by the Spirit you put to death the misdeeds of the body. . ." (Romans 8:13).

Chosen to be fruit bearers, not cute ornaments.

In Romans, Paul discusses the difference in the mindset of a sinful man and one who is living according to God's will:

> *Those who live according to the sinful nature have their minds set on what that nature desires; but those who live in accordance with the Spirit have their minds set on what the Spirit desires. The mind of sinful man is death, but the mind controlled by the Spirit is life and peace; the sinful mind is hostile to God. Those controlled by the sinful nature cannot please*

~ CHAPTER NINE ~

God. You, however, are controlled not by the sinful nature but by the Spirit, if the Spirit of God lives in you. (Romans 8:5-9)

In other words, when you let the Holy Spirit direct and empower you, the sinful nature can no longer control you. We are told: ". . .the Spirit intercedes for the saints [us] in accordance with God's will" (Romans 8:27, Comments in brackets added).

Day by day, with the Holy Spirit and the study of Scripture, we can learn to think and act more Christ-like so that, over time, we will eventually become all the Lord wants and expects us to be. Paul likens our walk with the Lord to a race:

. . .let us throw off everything that hinders and the sin that so easily entangles, and let us run with perseverance the race marked out for us. Let us fix our eyes on Jesus, the author and perfecter of our faith, who for the joy set before him endured the cross, scorning its shame, and sat down at the right hand of the throne of God. (Hebrews 12:1-2)

Yes, Christ is the author of our faith. He is the beginning of our faith, because through His own faith in the Father to resurrect Him, He willingly became a sacrifice for us. Seeing first Christ's example, we can then believe in His sacrifice to receive forgiveness and ultimately salvation for ourselves.

We are also now able to receive promises and blessings through Him:

Until now you have not asked for anything in my name. Ask and you will receive, and your joy will be complete. (John 16:24)

~ Starting Over ~

Yes, Christ is the perfecter of our faith because He manifests or brings to fruition what we have faith for. Ultimately, Christ is the finisher, the completer of our faith. Again, He has set the example and paved the way for us. He has reached the goal. Just as He is now seated at the right hand of the throne of God, we continue following His example to reach that very same goal:

> *To him who overcomes, I will give the right to sit with me on my throne, just as I overcame and sat down with my Father on his throne. (Revelation 3:21)*

The Apostle Paul said:

> *. . . But one thing I do: Forgetting what is behind and straining toward what is ahead, I press on toward the goal to win the prize for which God has called me heavenward in Christ Jesus. (Philippians 3:13-14)*

To summarize, we have seen that the promise comes first. Then, it is up to us to believe it in order to receive it. The completion or end result of our faith is the fulfillment of that promise. The beginning and the end, the start and the finish, the race and the goal – all draw our focus towards Jesus. Then, by accepting Christ and following His example, we become renewed in our minds. And, as a result, our way of life becomes more like His. On top of all that, the Holy Spirit comes to reside in us to help us along the way. How merciful and good, God is to us!

~ CHAPTER TEN ~

Moving Forward With Faith

When we begin to realize exactly who this God is we serve, we can begin to trust Him and love Him with all our hearts. He is not a fictitious character. He is not someone's whim or figment of imagination. He is not a gas or cloud or surge of energy. Nor is He some distant "something" that has no relevance to us.

Let's look for a moment at some of the attributions and characteristics of the Almighty God that we serve and worship, of the One we look to with faith:

> *To the Lord your God belong the heavens, even the highest heavens, the earth and everything in it. . .For the Lord your God is God of gods and Lord of lords, the great God, mighty and awesome, who shows no partiality and accepts*

~ CHAPTER TEN ~

no bribes. He defends the cause of the fatherless and the widow, and loves the alien, giving him food and clothing. (Deuteronomy 10:14, 17-18)

When I consider your heavens, the work of your fingers, the moon and the stars, which you have set in place, what is man that you are mindful of him. . . (Psalm 8:3-4)

The Lord has established his throne in heaven, and his kingdom rules over all. (Psalm 103:19)

Do you not know? Have you not heard? The Lord is the everlasting God, the Creator of the ends of the earth. He will not grow tired or weary, and his understanding no one can fathom. He gives strength to the weary and increases the power of the weak. . . . those who hope in the Lord will renew their strength. (Isaiah 40:28-31)

. . . I am he, I am he who will sustain you. I have made you and I will carry you; I will sustain you and I will rescue you. To whom will you compare me or count me equal? To whom will you liken me that we may be compared? (Isaiah 46:4-5)

. . .I am God, and there is no other; I am God, and there is none like me. I make known the end from the beginning, from ancient times, what is still to come. I say: My purpose will stand, and I will do all that I please. . . . What I have said, that will I bring about; what I have planned, that will I do. (Isaiah 46:9-11)

~ Moving Forward With Faith ~

Because of the Lord's great love we are not consumed, for his compassions never fail. They are new every morning; great is your faithfulness. (Lamentations 3:22-23)

Who is a God like you, who pardons sin and forgives the transgression of the remnant of his inheritance? You do not stay angry forever but delight to show mercy. (Micah 7:18)

Can you begin to see, to understand, to fathom, that the God we serve and love is the creator of all that we see and know. He is the Most High God, the Everlasting God, and the Lord Almighty.

Can you comprehend that the God of the universe loves you? He knows you as the individual you are, for no one else is exactly like you or ever will be. He wants to take care of you as loving parents take care of their children. He wants to be closer to you than a best friend. He is the greatest instructor you could have, mentoring you in the ways of wisdom and success. He is more loving than any lover, bestowing on you unconditional love, and calling you to be His bride.

Faith in the Awesome Power of God!

The writer of Hebrews tells us: "Now faith is being sure of what we hope for and certain of what we do not see" (Hebrews 11:1). This means we have faith by believing what God says, even when we don't see His answer yet. It means we look to God instead of focusing on the circumstances, even when they may seem overwhelming and we can't see a way out. Have faith in God's ability to bring deliverance. It's not necessary for you to shoulder any burden alone because God has promised that He will carry it for you – if you will only ask. God promises to help us overcome if we will only trust Him. Having faith in the mighty awesome power of God

~ CHAPTER TEN ~

brings His intervention into our lives. Expect what God has said to come to pass, and it will.

In Psalm 78:4-8, David warns us not to hold back from telling our children all the wonderful things the Lord has done for us and what He did for those that went before us. As each succeeding generation continues this tradition, the wonders God has done will perpetually be remembered. As a result of not forgetting these things, each generation will have the faith to put their trust in God and will keep His commandments. This, in turn, will bring blessings into their lives. Being armed with the knowledge of God and holding to a firm belief in Him, these generations won't end up like others in the past, who didn't receive all the blessings God had to offer them because of their lack of trust and faith in His awesome power.

Exchange your worry for God's Peace.

Without a Doubt!

But, there is one major obstacle that always gets in the way of faith – doubt! Yes, how quickly we can forget and then soon begin to question God's ability to manage our bad circumstances when things get rough in our lives. We begin to think such things as: "I can't do it! This is too much for me! What if what the Bible says is not true? God helps everyone else, but why should He help me? Miracles are not for today!"

"All right," you ask, "then just how do I get rid of doubt?" You go to the Lord in prayer and ask forgiveness for your unbelief. Then, with your eyes, you read the Word; with your ears you hear it; and, with your mouth you speak it. You continue doing this until the word is firmly planted in your mind and heart. It will then begin to grow in your spirit.

~ *Moving Forward With Faith* ~

Believing is what we do. It is the aggressive action of expecting God to show up at any moment and when you expect Him, He will show up. As long as you continue believing Him, God is working in your life.

Doubting in Action

A good example of a people who doubted is found in Psalm 78. In this example, David vividly illustrates the wonders God performed in bringing the people of Israel out of Egypt:

> *He divided the sea and led them through; he made the water stand firm like a wall. he guided them with the cloud by day and with light from the fire all night. He split the rocks in the desert and gave them water as abundant as the seas; he brought streams out of a rocky crag and made water flow down like rivers. (Psalm 78:13-16)*

But, if we look at this group of people from long ago, we find they had the same problem as we often do in dealing with this five-letter word – doubt – that brings hopelessness and despair. The fact is doubt and faith do not mix! Where there is doubt, there is no faith. Continuing on in the passage of Psalm 78, we learn that, even after witnessing these miracles, the Israelites still grumbled and complained:

> *They willfully put God to the test by demanding the food they craved. They spoke against God, saying, 'Can God spread a table in the desert? When he struck the rock, water gushed out, and streams flowed abundantly. But can he also give us food? Can he supply meat for his people?' (Psalm 78:18-20)*

~ CHAPTER TEN ~

Do you understand how the Israelites willfully tested God and spoke against Him? By the questions they asked, it is revealed that they just didn't understand God's great desire and awesome ability to take care of them. They continually responded by asking, "Can God . . . " or "But can he . . . " or "Can he . . . " What was their problem? Sad to say, the Psalm tells us that they "did not believe in God or trust in his deliverance" (Psalm 78:22). The writer of Hebrews tells us:

> *And without faith it is impossible to please God, because anyone who comes to him must believe that he exists and that he rewards those who earnestly seek him. (Hebrews 11:6)*

An unbelieving heart is called a sinful heart: "See to it brothers, that none of you has a sinful, unbelieving heart that turns away from the living God" (Hebrews 3:12). The Israelites of old are used as an example of warning: "So we see that they were not able to enter [the promised land], because of their unbelief" (Hebrews 3:19 Comment in brackets added).

At certain times in our lives, we all have difficulty with doubt. The key is in recognizing it and dealing with it immediately. When we have faith, we can know with confidence we will receive answers. So, how do you overcome feelings of doubt? When those first fleeting doubts cross your mind, go to the Bible and replace them with the Word of God. Remember who God is – He is the awesome, powerful, creator of the entire universe. Is He able? Of course He is able. But, does He want to hear from you and answer your prayers? Of course He does. He loves you! He wants you to have every good thing. And remember to fill your spirit continually with the Holy Spirit – on a daily basis, through the Word of God and through praise and worship and prayer. As you let the Holy Spirit permeate you, His power will help you replace that doubt with faith.

Faith Is Believing Without Doubting

When we believe without doubting and line ourselves up with God's will, we are then able to receive from Him. But, when we doubt, we tie God's hands, and He will not be able to bless us as much as He would like to. Because of His great mercy and love, He will often bless us and intervene for us despite ourselves. But, doubt and unbelief can actually keep away miracles. "And he [Jesus] did not do many miracles there because of their lack of faith" (Matthew 13:58 Comment in brackets added). The reality is that if you aren't really expecting anything, you really aren't believing. Faith is believing without doubting.

On the other hand, when we have faith and believe the Word of God – we can ask anything of the Father that is within His will and know with confidence that we will receive it. John tells us:

> *This is the confidence we have in approaching God: that if we ask anything according to his will, he hears us – whatever we ask – we know that we have what we asked of him. (1 John 5:14)*

Stepping Out in Faith

Let's look at an example that Peter gives us of what faith, as well as doubt, can do in our lives. Jesus had sent his disciples to go on ahead of Him to the other side of the lake, while He went up the mountainside to spend some time alone in prayer. By evening the boat was already about half way across the lake and the wind had become stronger. So "Jesus went out to them, walking on the lake" (Matthew 14:25). What

Faith is "right believing."

~ CHAPTER TEN ~

an awesome display that was of His authority and power to rule over the laws of creation. It was said: "You rule over the surging sea; when its waves mount up, you still them" (Psalm 89:9). When the disciples saw someone walking out on the water they were terrified to say the least. "But Jesus immediately said to them: 'Take courage! It is I. Don't be afraid' " (Matthew 14:27).

Peter, being brave said, "Lord, if it's you. . . tell me to come to you on the water" (Matthew 14:28). And, Jesus replied to His friend, "Come. . . Then Peter got down out of the boat, walked on the water and came toward Jesus" (Matthew 14:29). Peter through faith literally walked on water. But, the recounting of his experience continues:

> "...when he saw the wind, he was afraid and, beginning to sink, cried out, 'Lord, save me!' Immediately Jesus reached out his hand and caught him. 'You of little faith,' he said, 'why did you doubt?' (Matthew 14:30-31)

Yes, Peter was literally taking a giant leap of faith in this instance. With total faith in His Friend and Master, Peter walked out to meet Jesus. As long as his eyes remained on Jesus, he was fine. But, as soon as he looked around and saw the waves and felt the winds – the circumstances – doubt settled in, and he became frightened. Certainly, Peter must have also thought to himself, "I am not suppose to be able to do this." And, as he took his focus off the Lord just for a moment, he started to sink into the water.

We should always remember Peter's experience. It encourages us to keep our eyes off our circumstances and focused where they belong – on Jesus and His Word.

Henry Ford unknowingly summed up Peter's experience when he said, "Whether you think that you can, or that you can't, you are usually right."

Results of Negative Thoughts

When we hold onto negative thoughts and beliefs, we tend to find ourselves staying in a negative situation or drawing to ourselves that negative circumstance we really didn't want.

This happens, because when we doubt, we open ourselves up to attack from the enemy. Remember, Job said: "What I feared has come upon me; what I dreaded has happened to me" (Job 3:25). Our unbelief – our doubts – cause us to lose the "covering" of God. And when we aren't sensitive to the promptings of the Holy Spirit, then we allow Satan to work in our lives through our negative thoughts and words. Doubting is faith in your enemy.

A Phony?

The illustration of the fig tree is given to us by Mark:

> *The next day as they were leaving Bethany, Jesus was hungry. Seeing in the distance a fig tree in leaf, he went to find out if it had any fruit. When he reached it, he found nothing but leaves, because it was not the season for figs. Then he said to the tree, 'May no one ever eat fruit from you again.' And his disciples heard him say it. (Mark. 11:12-14)*

Normally, when a fig tree is full of leaves it is an indication that it is full of fruit. This fig tree had its leaves, but no figs. Looking at the tree allegorically, you could say it represented hypocrisy. It was pretending to be something it wasn't – it was a phony. Do we say we love God, yet doubt His Word? Let's not be phonies? If we love Him then we should trust Him and believe His word. Having faith in God brings His intervention into our lives and it pleases Him: "And without faith it is impossible to please God. . ." (Hebrews 11:6).

~ CHAPTER TEN ~

Faith's Power

The morning following the incident with Jesus and the fig tree, the disciples discovered the tree had withered from its roots. Remembering what Jesus had said to the tree, Peter pointed it out to Him. Jesus' answer gives us a mighty example of the power of faith:

> *Have faith in God. I tell you the truth, if anyone says to this mountain, 'Go, throw yourself into the sea,' and does not doubt in his heart but believes that what he says will happen, it will be done for him. (Mark 11:22-23)*

These "mountains" can represent the problems that come into our lives. Do your problems seem like mountains to you sometimes – no way to get over it, through it or around it, or just overwhelming in magnitude?

The fig tree was a problem that came into Jesus' life. He expected to find fruit on it so that He could satisfy His hunger, but it didn't have any. Seeing the tree's leaves from a distance, it had also deceived Him, making Him think it was fruitful. His reaction to this problem was to speak to it. The next day the fig tree – the problem – was gone. Jesus removed that problem, that deception, that unfruitful thing out of the way – out of His life, by speaking to it.

In the same way Jesus spoke to this problem that came into His life, we can speak to the problems that come into our lives – those things that are deceptions, those things that are unfruitful, and tell them to "Go" (Mark 11:23). Let that thing, that situation, that problem – your fig tree or mountain – know that it no longer has any control over you because you have given the Lord full control to work in that circumstance.

By faith in the power of God, speak believing those things will be removed from your life. When you ask in prayer with faith, it will be done for you:

~ Moving Forward With Faith ~

> *Therefore I tell you, whatever you ask for in prayer, believe that you have received it, and it will be yours. (Mark 11:24)*

Yes! Through faith and prayer, mountains are removed. Alone, we are helpless, and circumstances can make life look hopeless, "... but with God all things are possible" (Matthew 19:26).

A Mighty Example of Intervention

In Luke 8:40-55, there is the account of Jairus who came to Jesus pleading with Him to come to his home and heal his only daughter. She was just twelve and lay dying. But, as Jesus went with Jairus, another situation came up that required His immediate attention. Poor Jairus had to wait patiently as Jesus lingered, knowing at any moment his daughter could pass away.

What would you do in such a situation? How would you feel? Waiting for Jesus, Jairus probably felt nervous and frustrated, wanting Him to hurry before it was too late. Then, while Jesus was taking care of this other matter, someone from Jairus' house came and met them. "... 'Your daughter is dead,' he said. 'Don't bother the teacher anymore'" (Luke 8:49).

What a horrible thing to be told! But, ignoring the message these men brought, Jesus said to His friend: "... Don't be afraid; just believe and she will be healed" (Luke 8:50). But, this must have been difficult for Jairus to believe. And, when they arrived at his house, all the people were wailing and mourning for his daughter:

> ... *'Stop wailing,' Jesus said. 'She is not dead but asleep.' They laughed at him, knowing that she was dead. But he took her by the hand and said, 'My child, get up!' Her spirit*

~ CHAPTER TEN ~

returned, and at once she stood up. Then Jesus told them to give her something to eat. (Luke 8:52-55)

Oh, what a wonderful ending, I felt like clapping and praising God. Even though the circumstances were as bad as they could get; Jesus turned everything around. In the same way, He can breathe life back into a situation in which you can see no hope. There is no circumstance He can't remedy.

God Can Make a Difference

Is there a situation in your life today that you feel or think is hopeless, and you feel like giving up or you are losing hope? Having the knowledge that Jesus can breathe life back into that situation will turn your feelings of hopelessness, discouragement, and despair into a deep abiding faith and hope in knowing that no matter what the circumstance, God can make a difference.

So I want to say to you as Jesus said to Jairus, "Don't be afraid, just believe," and healing will come, circumstances will change. You might not know when, but it will be in God's perfect timing. You may have to exercise and develop your patience. And, maybe it won't be the way you expected, but it will happen.

With great expectation, you can depend on God to perform a miracle or give you the ability to get through the bad circumstances that come into your life and to overcome them. Be encouraged by knowing: ". . . that in all things God works for the good of those who love him, who have been called according to his purpose" (Romans 8:28). Without a doubt, you can have the confidence to believe and trust in the Lord.

~ CHAPTER ELEVEN ~

Taking Action

*I*t's exciting to serve a living, active, loving God:

> *Know therefore that the Lord your God is God; he is the faithful God, keeping his covenant of love to a thousand generations of those who love him and keep his commands. (Deuteronomy 7:9)*

Give the Lord full rein and let Him work in your life by believing in Him. Know what's in your Bible – know what the Word of God says. Then, don't believe the circumstance, but believe God. Let God be God in every circumstance. I thank Him that He is a loving, Heavenly Father who cares about every detail of our lives – yours and mine. Yes, it's true – "Jesus Christ is the same yesterday and today and forever" (Hebrews 13:8). If God intervened and performed miracles in the lives of people in the "old days," we know He is still doing the same today!

Believing Is Action

The dictionary tells us the word "believing" means "having a firm conviction as to the reality or goodness of something." So then, believing isn't "hoping" something will happen or take place – it is "knowing" it will. When people believe, God reacts, and He doesn't care who you are, what your background is or where you came from. Peter tells us:

> . . .*I now realize how true it is that God does not show favoritism but accepts men from every nation who fear him and do what is right. (Acts 10:34-35)*

You see, what God does for one person, He can also do for you. That's because He loves us all the same. But, this doesn't mean we look for God to do everything for us that we saw Him do in someone else's life. No, that shouldn't be our focus. Our focus should always be towards God and exerting our faith in His word, so we can see it manifested in our own lives.

Now, there is a time when God *gives* us a certain measure of faith. We find this faith explained by Paul:

> . . .*Do not think of yourself more highly than you ought, but rather think of yourself with sober judgment, in accordance with the measure of faith God has given you. . . . in Christ we who are many form one body, and each member belongs to all the others. We have different gifts, according to the grace given us." (Romans 12:3, 5, 6)*

~ Taking Action ~

This faith refers to the power God gives each believer to fulfill his or her ministry in the church. Since it comes from God, there can be no reason for a self-righteous attitude.

But, how do we receive more of the faith that allows us to trust God and to believe His word? Paul gives us the answer: ". . .faith comes from hearing the message, and the message is heard through the word of Christ" (Romans 10:17). We grow in faith by focusing on the Word of God, His promises and what He has already done.

The writer of Hebrews tells us:

> *For we also have had the gospel preached to us, just as they [the Israelites] did; but the message they heard was of no value to them, because those who heard did not combine it with faith. (Hebrews 4:2, Comments in brackets added)*

Is this a paradox? Are these contradictory verses? James clears it up for us:

> *"What good is it. . .if a man claims to have faith but has no deeds? Can such faith save him? . . . faith by itself, if it is not accompanied by action, is dead. . .I will show you my faith by what I do." (James 2:14, 17, 18)*

James also tells us: "Do not merely listen to the word, and so deceive yourselves. Do what it says" (James 1:22). So we learn having faith involves action. When we believe God and trust in His word, our faith will cause us to think differently, to speak differently, and to act differently. Faith is not abstract, it is real: "Faith is the substance of things hoped for, the evidence of things not seen" (Hebrews 11:1 KJV).

~ CHAPTER ELEVEN ~

Often in Scripture and especially throughout the New Testament, we are encouraged to do good things – those things that are pleasing to God. At the same time, it is impressed upon us that doing right doesn't earn us salvation or God's favor, because that can come only through Jesus Christ. It's what Christ did and our faith in Him as our Savior and not our obedience to the law that saves us. On the other hand, when we are obedient to God's ways, we glorify Him and please Him.

> *Your content is more important than your container.*

In a passage in Galatians we find the Apostle Paul explaining that those who keep the law to receive justification or in order to become righteous enough to be worthy of salvation won't find it. It can't happen. Then, in Galatians 5:6, he goes on to say: ". . .the only thing that counts is faith expressing itself through love." Having faith is expressed in acts of love. God expressed His love for us through His grace – by redeeming us through the shed blood of His Son. As a result of accepting His love for us, we, in turn, go out and express love towards others. This passage continues with this instruction:

> *You, my brothers, were called to be free. But do not use your freedom to indulge the sinful nature; rather, serve one another in love. The entire law is summed up in a single command: 'Love your neighbor as yourself.' (Galatians 5:13-14)*

Approaching God With Confidence

When we have faith in God's word, we are then able to pray with a believing heart, without doubting. Jesus said: "If you believe, you will receive whatever you ask for in prayer"

(Matthew 21:22). So we must believe, God can do and will do what we ask.

James, the brother of Jesus, gives us this valuable insight into the "mystery" of "unanswered" prayer:

> *But when he asks, he must believe and not doubt, because he who doubts is like a wave of the sea, blown and tossed by the wind. That man should not think he will receive anything from the Lord; he is a double-minded man, unstable in all he does. (James 1:6-8)*

It is also important to have the right motives when we come before God in prayer. Our desires must be pure, and they cannot be pure if we ask according to our own selfish wants. James goes on to tell us:

> *When you ask, you do not receive, because you ask with wrong motives, that you may spend what you get on your pleasures. (James 4:3)*

Many people don't realize this when they go to the Lord in prayer and that is why they don't always get the answer they expect. When this happens to you, it's time to re-examine your motives.

It is also wise to examine our lives on a regular basis – our thoughts and our actions. Do we have any unrepentant sin that we are holding on to? The Psalmist tells us: "If I had cherished sin in my heart, the Lord would not have listened" (Psalm 66:18). When we continue in sin, we quickly find ourselves outside the will of God. Then, the question is, "Why should we expect the Lord to give us what we ask for, if we

Leave Godly imprints on the lives of others.

~ CHAPTER ELEVEN ~

are deliberately not obedient and faithful to Him?" Instead, have a repentant heart by recognizing any sin in your life and asking God to forgive you of that sin. Then follow the instruction Jesus gave the adulteress when He told her: ". . . Go now and leave your life of sin" (John 8:11).

Taking this kind of inventory of your life is not to make you feel prideful if you think you are doing everything right, and it is not to make you feel down if you think you just keep doing everything wrong. Our focus should always be towards Jesus, who is merciful and loving, and so worthy of our praise and worship.

Yes, our high priest, Jesus Christ, understands our weakness because He was also tempted in every way, but He never gave in to those temptations. Yet, He is always ready to help us when we are tempted. The writer of Hebrews encourages us:

> *Let us then approach the throne of grace with confidence, so that we may receive mercy and find grace to help us in our time of need. (Hebrews 4:16)*

Also remember, when you ask forgiveness for those things that might slip into your life, you can know without a doubt that you are no longer held accountable for them. The price has already been paid and God has pronounced a verdict of not guilty on you:

> *Who is he that condemns? Christ Jesus, who died – more than that, who was raised to life – is at the right hand of God and is also interceding for us. (Romans 8:34)*

John adds:

> *. . .if our hearts do not condemn us, we have confidence before God and receive from him*

> *anything we ask, because we obey his commands and do what pleases him. And this is his command: to believe in the name of his Son, Jesus Christ, and to love one another as he commanded us. (1 John 3:21-23)*

Praying God's Will

John gives us input with this verse:

> *This is the confidence we have in approaching God: that if we ask anything according to* His will, *he hears us. (1 John 5:14)*

According to this scripture, we must learn to ask for those things that we know are in the Father's will. And how do we find out what His will is? We search His word, where His will is revealed to us. Again, Christ set the example: "For I have come down from heaven not to do my will but to do the will of him who sent me" (John 6:38).

As our minds are renewed and as we begin to pattern our thinking after God's, we will know "what God's will is – his good, pleasing and perfect will" (Romans 12:2). In Ephesians, we are also told to:

> *"Be very careful, then, how you live – not as unwise but as wise. . . do not be foolish, but understand what the Lord's will is." (Ephesians 5:15,17)*

Knowing God's will is knowing His purposes for you and knowing His purpose for mankind. We learn in His Word:

> *. . .he chose us in him before the creation of the world to be holy and blameless in his sight. In love he predestined us to be adopted as his*

› *sons through Jesus Christ, in accordance with his pleasure and will – to the praise of his glorious grace . . . And he made known to us the mystery of his will . . . to be put into effect when the times will have reached their fulfillment – to bring all things in heaven and on earth together under one head, even Christ. In him we were also chosen. . . in order that we, who were the first to hope in Christ, might be for the praise of his glory. (Ephesians 1:4-6, 9-12)*

As followers of Christ, we glorify God by learning to live pure and blameless lives with the help of the Holy Spirit. In the same way, the things that we pray for should ultimately result in the glorifying of God.

Asking in the Name of Jesus

Asking in the name of Jesus completes our prayers. Jesus said: " . . . I tell you the truth, my Father will give you whatever you ask in my name" (John 16:23). Paul tells us:

> *. . . God exalted him [Jesus] to the highest place and gave him the name that is above every name, that at the name of Jesus every knee should bow, in heaven and on earth and under the earth, and every tongue confess that Jesus Christ is Lord, to the glory of God the Father. (Philippians 2:9-11, Comments in brackets added)*

Using the name of Jesus refers to the position and authority He has been given. His name is above every name – whatever you can name, Jesus Christ has authority over it. For instance, He has authority over anger, over depression, over cancer, over any sin you can name, over any disease you can name, and over anything else you can name. Just name your trouble and take it to the Lord. Paul tells us: ". . . in all things we are more than conquerors through him [Christ] who loved us" (Romans 8:37, Comments in brackets added).

You have now been given some keys for effective prayer. Remember that God always responds to your prayers. It's just that sometimes His answer is not the one you may have been hoping to receive. But, for the most effective prayers believe, without doubting, that you will receive an answer, ask with the right motives, have a repentant heart, obey His commands by loving Him and one another, ask according to His will, and use the authority that comes from the name of Jesus. How can you help but to have victory in your life when Jesus is interceding for you in the heavenly realm and the Holy Spirit is in you giving you power to overcome in the physical realm. Yes, the greatest power in the universe is on your side!

Putting God's Purposes First

Now, what if you have done all these things that have been mentioned and you still had to walk through a fiery trial, or someone you prayed for wasn't healed or even died? Do you let doubt settle in again? Do you let those negative thoughts creep back in that say, "God doesn't care"? Do friends begin to question your faith and make you feel even worse?

Let's look at an example from the life of Jesus. Jesus knew the scriptures that prophesied the Savior's death. Those scriptures not only prophesied His death, but also the physical torture that would leave Him unrecognizable. To be whipped and beaten to such a degree is not something He would want

You are what you eat – so start feeding on the Word.

~ CHAPTER ELEVEN ~

to look forward to. To hang on a cross with nails pounded into His hands and pounded into His feet, His chest heaving with each breath under the weight of His own body resting on the nail that tore the flesh from His feet would not be something He would want to think about.

Jesus' only crime was the love He had for people, His desire to bring healing to them, and to give them the knowledge of a loving, caring Heavenly Father Who wanted to fellowship with them. He went about performing miracles, wonders, and signs, proving Himself to be the Messiah.

To face the immense pain and gruesome death that He knew was ahead was not easy for Him. He took it to the Father in prayer:

> *'Father, if you are willing, take this cup [the suffering that was to come] from me; yet not my will, but yours be done'. . . And being in anguish, he prayed more earnestly, and his sweat was like drops of blood falling to the ground. (Luke 22:42, 44)*

In extreme cases of anguish or strain, sweat and blood have been known to mingle together. This phenomenon is known as hematidrosis. Jesus prayed with such intense emotion that drops of blood literally came through the pores of His body. Have you ever prayed until you sweated drops of blood?

Paraphrasing His prayer, He was pleading, "Please, if I don't have to go through this, if there can be another way, let it be so. Never the less, I'll do whatever you require of me."

Yes, Jesus prayed in faith, believing, and without sin in His life. But He also prayed for the Father's will to be done, "yet not my will, but yours be done." In praying this way, He would know that whatever happened, it would bring about the desired result to fulfill God's plans. He was willing to submit to the Father's will, even if it meant He would not get the deliverance He sought from what was about to take place in His life.

~ Taking Action ~

Was Jesus' request – to avoid the persecution and death He knew was coming – answered? Was He delivered from this trial? Certainly, if anyone could come before the Father believing with total faith for His answer, it would have been Jesus Christ. But, despite His prayers and plea, He still had to face that trial, and He still had to endure it.

Are you going to point a finger at Jesus and say, "Well, He didn't have enough faith, or He must have doubted, or He had sin in His life?" Of course not! Most importantly, Jesus was willing to pray that the Father's will be done over His own desires. So you see, praying in faith doesn't always mean you will have *your* petitions fulfilled, but it will guarantee that God's is fulfilled.

When God's answer is, "No," that means He has a better plan and a better purpose. And, there was a greater purpose to come from the death of Jesus Christ. He may have had to suffer and die despite His prayers, but He also *won* victory over sin and death for *all* of mankind! He was resurrected from the dead and now lives in power and authority at the right hand of God the Father!

Suffering for Christ

There have been times in the history of the church where our brothers and sisters in the Lord have been called upon to go through persecution and to ultimately give their very lives for their faith in Jesus. To the martyred church of Smyrna, the Lord said:

> *Do not be afraid of what you are about to suffer. I tell you, the devil will put some of you in prison to test you, and you will suffer persecution for ten days. Be faithful, even to the point of death, and I will give you the crown of life. (Revelation 2:10)*

~ CHAPTER ELEVEN ~

There are areas in the world today where those who have put their faith in Jesus are still being tortured and killed for their belief in Him. It is written:

> *Whatever happens, conduct yourselves in a manner worthy of the gospel of Christ. . . . without being frightened in any way by those who oppose you. This is a sign to them that they will be destroyed, but that you will be saved – and that by God. For it has been granted to you on behalf of Christ not only to believe on him, but also to suffer for him. (Philippians 1:27-29)*

There is also a time yet to come, just before the return of Christ to this earth, when the church again as a whole will be persecuted, and many will be asked to give their life for their God, for the One who was first willing to sacrifice His life for them. But Paul states:

> *I consider that our present sufferings are not worth comparing with the glory that will be revealed in us. (Romans 8:18)*

When you have prayed in faith, then you know your part has been done and God is now in control of what you prayed about. So, even if the answer is different than what you desired, remember God sees the whole picture, the complete picture from beginning to the end. And, what is done will be what He knows is best for that situation. He has a plan for your life and the end result will be according to His will, if you have prayed even as Jesus did: ". . . Yet not as I will, but as you will" (Matthew 26:39). The writer of Hebrews tells us:

> *. . . do not throw away your confidence; it will be richly rewarded. You need to persevere so*

~ Taking Action ~

that when you have done the will of God, you will receive what he has promised. (Hebrews 10:35-36)

Matthew calls the persecuted blessed:

Blessed are those who are persecuted because of righteousness, for theirs is the kingdom of heaven. (Matthew 5:10)

The Apostle Peter adds this encouragement:

But rejoice that you participate in the sufferings of Christ, so that you may be overjoyed when his glory is revealed...if you suffer as a Christian, do not be ashamed, but praise God that you bear that name. (1 Peter 4:13, 16)

Again, follow Jesus' example if you want the best for your life. Pray with faith but also be willing to say, "May Your will be done." Let your goal be – finding the will of God for your life. He offers us so many blessings and benefits now, but our greatest reward is eternal life with Him.

~ CHAPTER TWELVE ~

My Heart Speaks

Our speech is a very significant controlling factor in our lives. The power of our words are greater than we realize. Does your speech stop you from being all God wants you to be?

The writer of Hebrews tells us: ". . .the word of God is living and active. . ." (Hebrews 4:12). Through Isaiah the Lord tells us:

> *. . .so is my word that goes out from my mouth: It will not return to me empty, but will accomplish what I desire and achieve the purpose for which I sent it. (Isaiah 55:11)*

From the Psalmist, we are told about the creative power of the word that comes forth from God:

~ CHAPTER TWELVE ~

*By the word of the Lord were the heavens made,
their starry host by the breath of his mouth...
For he spoke, and it came to be; he commanded,
and it stood firm. (Psalm 33:6, 9)*

God has said we are made in His image. And, just as He is a creative God, He has given us creative abilities as well. Just as He creates with the words He speaks, we are told through His Word that our words also have this ability. Our words have spiritual power even though they come out of a physical mouth: "The tongue has the power of life and death. . ." (Proverbs 18:21).

Careless Words

Are you careful with the words you speak? The Bible tells us there is power in the tongue, and we should be careful in how we use it. We should "say what we mean and mean what we say." In other words, it would be best if we would always think before we speak. Remember that God is very concerned about what we say. Jesus warns us that we will all have to "give [an] account on the day of judgment for every careless word [we] have spoken" (Matthew 12:36, Comments in brackets added).

Isaiah understood this. When he saw the Lord in a vision, he knew immediately how imperfect and unworthy he was to be in the presence of God. Receiving a glimpse of the Lord's throne was an experience that changed his entire perspective on life. He realized that, for him, one of the first things that needed "fixing" was his way of speaking. When he saw the Lord in all His glory seated on the throne, Isaiah lamented:

> *'Woe to me!' he cried. 'I am ruined! For I am a man of unclean lips, and I live among a people of unclean lips, and my eyes have seen the King, the Lord Almighty.' (Isaiah 6:5)*

~ My Heart Speaks ~

How We Talk Is Important

The following scriptures again emphasize that God is very concerned about how we speak:

> *The Lord detests lying lips, but He delights in men who are truthful. (Proverbs 12:22)*

> *Do not let any unwholesome talk come out of your mouths, but only what is helpful for building others up according to their needs, that it may benefit those who listen. (Ephesians 4:29)*

> *Nor should there be obscenity, foolish talk or coarse joking, which are out of place, but rather thanksgiving. (Ephesians 5:4)*

> *Do everything without complaining or arguing. (Philippians 2:14)*

You see, the Lord is pure and holy in every way. As believers in Christ, we are to set our sights on Jesus as our inspiration. In every way, we are to live our lives by His example.

Words Can Do All That?

Sometimes we don't realize the true power and effect our words can have on our own lives – as well as on the lives of others. Let's look at a few examples from Scripture:

> *Reckless words pierce like a sword, but the tongue of the wise brings healing. (Proverbs 12:18)*

> *An anxious heart weighs a man down, but a kind word cheers him up. (Proverbs 12:25)*

~ CHAPTER TWELVE ~

A gentle answer turns away wrath, but a harsh word stirs up anger. (Proverbs 15:1)

An honest answer is like a kiss on the lips. (Proverbs 24:26)

A word aptly spoken is like apples of gold in settings of silver. (Proverbs 25:11)

Pleasant words are a honeycomb, sweet to the soul and healing to the bones. (Proverbs 16:24)

Your Words Project Your Life

Our words can even be a self-fulfilling prophecy. Yes, it's true. That's why what you speak or think about most is what you often "attract" to yourself – whether it be good or bad. Solomon tells us: " The mouth of the righteous is a fountain of life, but violence overwhelms the mouth of the wicked" (Proverbs 10:11) and "He who guards his lips guards his life, but he who speaks rashly will come to ruin" (Proverbs 13:3).

The apostle Paul puts it this way:

> *. . .A man reaps what he sows. The one who sows to please his sinful nature, from that nature will reap destruction; the one who sows to please the Spirit, from the Spirit will reap eternal life. (Galatians 6:7-8)*

This example of the principle of sowing and reaping shows that it applies negatively as well as positively. Looking at this principle from the negative side, Proverbs tells us: "An evil man is trapped by his sinful talk. . ." (Proverbs 12:13). Jesus adds:

~ My Heart Speaks ~

> . . . 'What comes out of a man is what makes him 'unclean.' For from within, out of men's hearts, come evil thoughts, sexual immorality, theft, murder, adultery, greed, malice, deceit, lewdness, envy, slander, arrogance and folly. All these evils come from inside and make a man 'unclean.' (Mark 7:20-23)

From these verses we see that wrong thoughts cause unrighteous speech which creates or leads to evil actions. In Proverbs, we learn that the reverse is also true: "From the fruit of his lips a man is filled with good things as surely as the work of his hands rewards him" (Proverbs 12:14). In other words, just as a person reaps a harvest from the work he does with his hands, he also reaps a harvest from the words he speaks. When good things are spoken, then he will reap good things in his life. Jesus further illustrates this concept by telling us:

You are influenced by those around you, so start hanging out with God.

> The good man brings good things out of the good stored up in his heart, and the evil man brings evil things out of the evil stored up in his heart. For out of the overflow of his heart his mouth speaks. (Luke 6:45)

The results are that the thoughts and words of a good man can bring good into his life while the thoughts and words of an evil man can bring evil into his life.

Focus on Good Things!

The evangelist Joyce Meyer says, "What you focus on is what develops in your life." The evangelist Cleflo Dollar tells us,

~ CHAPTER TWELVE ~

"What you believe is what controls your life." What both are saying is that "poor vision equals a poor life" and "negative vision equals a negative life" while "good vision equals a good life." Pastor Casey Treat puts it this way: "How you set your mind will determine life or death; in your home, in your finances, in your life."

That wonderful motivational speaker and author, Zig Ziglar tells us: "The only way to change where you are is to change your mind. You are the sum total of your thoughts up to this point in your life. If you keep thinking what you've been thinking, you will keep getting what you've been getting." The writer and evangelist, Mike Murdock, shortens Zig Ziglar's point by saying, "What you expect comes toward you."

Today more and more people are beginning to understand what the Bible has taught all along. The world understands the "principle of positive thinking." Do they realize this concept is based on a principle that God set in motion from the beginning of creation? In Proverbs we are told that there is life and death in our words – positive words bring life and negative words bring death. We must also understand that we can only truly be positive when we know God and who we are in Him. It is through understanding the heart of God that our fears and doubts can be turned to trust and faith in Him.

Speaking the Word

Can you truly say, "Nobody loves me" when the Word of God tells you:

> ...*neither height nor depth, nor anything else in all creation, will be able to separate us from the love of God that is in Christ Jesus our Lord. (Romans 8:39)*

~ My Heart Speaks ~

Can you truly say, "I can't forgive myself – I feel so guilty" when the Word of God tells you: "If we confess our sins, he is faithful and just and will forgive us our sins and purify us from all unrighteousness" (1 John 1:9) and ". . .there is now no condemnation for those who are in Christ Jesus" (Romans 8:1).

Can you truly say, "I am so afraid this will happen or that will happen" when the Word of God tells you:

> *Peace I leave with you; my peace I give you. . . . Do not let your hearts be troubled and do not be afraid." (John 14:27)*

Can you truly say, "I'm worried" when the Word of God tells you:

> *Cast all you anxiety on him because he cares for you. (1 Peter 5:7)*

Can you truly say, "I'm lonely" when the Word of God tells you:

> *. . . 'Never will I leave you; never will I forsake you.' (Hebrews 13:5)*

It is time to stand firmly on God's word. The Psalmist said of the Lord: "All your words are true, . . ." (Psalm 119:160). We can depend on God. Let's speak His Word. Paul sums it all up for us with these instructions:

> *And whatever you do, whether in word or deed, do it all in the name of the Lord Jesus, giving thanks to God the Father through him. (Colossians 3:17)*

Yes, we should let everything we do and say glorify the Lord. But how can mere words be so important? Don't forget that God created the world by speaking words! And, He gave

~ CHAPTER TWELVE ~

the words we would speak spiritual power as well – even the ". . .power of life and death. . ." (Proverbs 18:21).

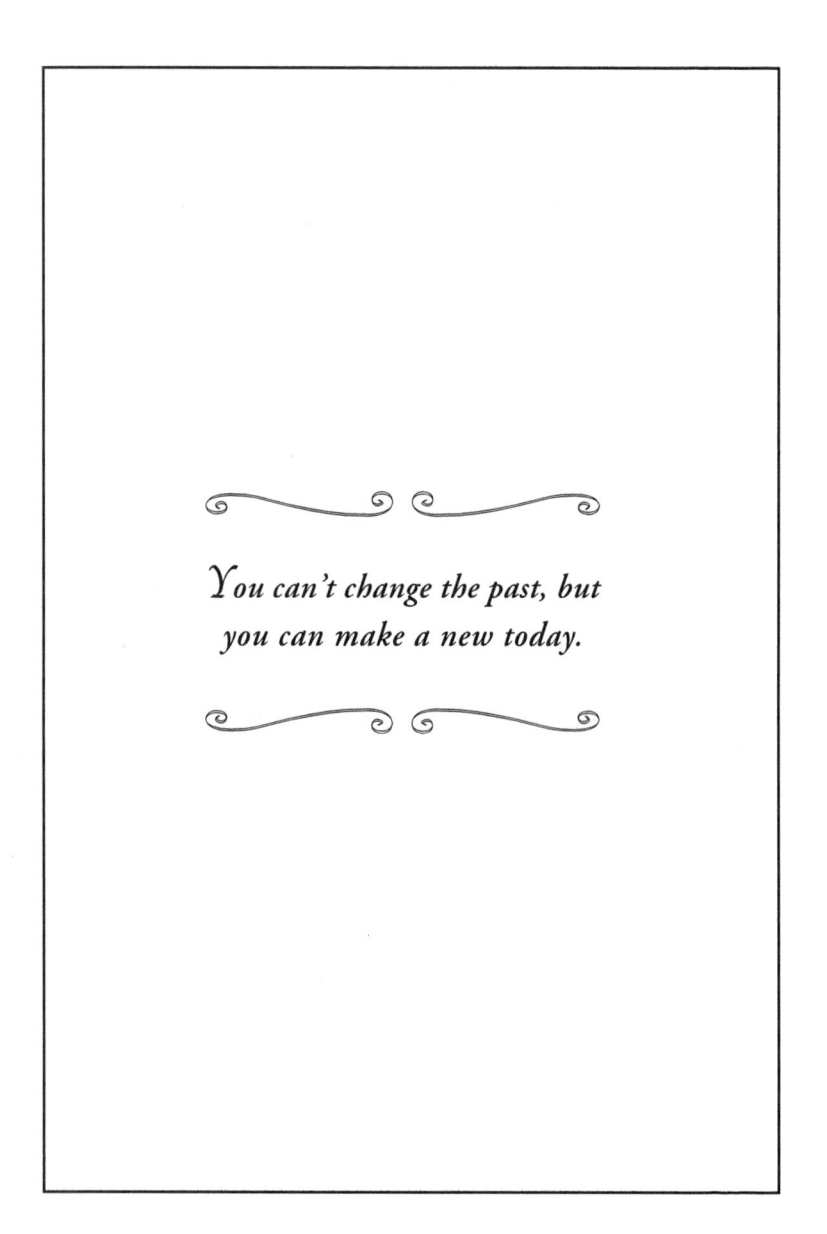

You can't change the past, but you can make a new today.

~ CHAPTER THIRTEEN ~

Living in Blessings

In my study of the Scriptures, I began to see that often when a promise or blessing was offered, it also came with an "if you" or a "when you." There was a choice and a decision to be made. In Deuteronomy, there is a good illustration of this:

> . . .*I have set before you life and death, blessings and curses. Now* choose *life, so that you and your children may live and that you may love the Lord your God, listen to his voice, and hold fast to him.* (Deuteronomy 30:19)

He wants us to choose the way of blessings, not curses. He wants us to choose the way that brings life. I can't count how many times I have cried out to God reminding Him of His promises and blessings, wondering why I didn't see them

~ CHAPTER THIRTEEN ~

come to fruition in my life. Here in Deuteronomy, God is telling us that a condition or requirement has to be met in order to receive those promises and blessings. Even more, we have a choice as to whether or not to adhere to those conditions.

So, what is a "condition"? It means God requires something of each of us before He will release His blessings. I have learned to search my life and see "if" and "when" I have fulfilled His condition or conditions. If, after my soul-searching, I find that I haven't met God's conditions in my life, then I begin putting into practice what He has requested. Sure enough, once I meet those "conditions," the blessings follow. It would be good for all of us to go through the Bible and pick out all the "if you" and "when you" parts and make sure we're following God's precepts.

A good illustration of this is a parent saying to his child: "After you clean up your room, you may go play baseball with your friends." Now if the child chooses not to clean up his room, then he can't expect the reward or fulfillment of the blessing to be able to play with his friends. Why? Because the condition wasn't met. Similarly, a parent can tell a child: "When you are sixteen and have passed the driver's test, you may drive the car." A fourteen-year old can beg and cry and beseech his parents to drive the car, but the parents will remain adamant in their decision. Why? Because the conditions for driving have not been met. When the child is sixteen and has passed the driving test, then and only then will he be allowed to drive the car because now he has met all the conditions that had been stipulated.

God's Training School

Besides giving awards, parents also discipline their children to help train and teach them. For example, if a child, unwilling to follow directions, continues in an undesirable behavior, a negative reaction from a good parent will follow. On the other hand, if the child continues in a good behavior, a positive reaction will follow from the parent. In this way, a child learns through experience what to do and what not to do - what is appropriate behavior and what is not appropriate. In other words, the child learns the difference between "right" and "wrong." So, it is in this same manner that God as a loving father deals with all of His children.

Just because we finally learn one lesson, it does not mean the training stops there. God continues teaching us through our life experiences and through His word. In Proverbs, we learn that: ". . . the Lord disciplines those He loves" (Proverbs 3:12). In Hebrews, the writer also tells us:

> . . . God disciplines us for our good, that we may share in his holiness. No discipline seems pleasant at the time, but painful. Later on, however, it produces a harvest of righteousness and peace for those who have been trained by it. (Hebrews 12:10-11)

How good and great God is! He offers us a system of rewards just as we do for our own children. When we fulfill the conditions He has set in advance, we receive His blessings automatically. You see, there is no need to cry and beg or question why they haven't been received.

Just as there are physical laws set in motion, there are also spiritual laws that have been set into motion. For example, if we let go of an object we are holding, it will fall to the ground. This is called the "law of gravity" – what goes up, must come down. Spiritual laws work in much the same way. When we fall in line with them, we receive blessings. When we don't follow them or oppose them, God tells us that curses will follow, giving us just the opposite of what we desire.

When we accepted Christ as our Savior, that first step was not a physical action. It came from our heart and mind. Then,

~ CHAPTER THIRTEEN ~

it was followed by spoken words expressing that acceptance of Him. The promise of "forgiveness of sins" from the Lord followed. But, our hearts and words had to line up first with God's will which was to except His son as our Lord and Savior. We will receive all that God has to offer -- all His promises and all His blessings when we have faith in Him, believe His word, and follow His ways. What great expectations we can have when we accept Jesus as our Savior!

Keep in mind that our works won't get us into heaven. Salvation is deliverance from the final results of sin which is death. Only through the grace of Jesus Christ can we receive the free gift of eternal life. And, what is expected of us? Only that we accept Jesus Christ as our Lord and personal Savior, believing in Him:

> *For it is by grace you have been saved, through faith – and this not from yourselves, it is the gift of God – not by works, so that no one can boast. For we are God's workmanship, created in Christ Jesus to do good works, which God prepared in advance for us to do. (Ephesians 2:8-10)*

Even though we can't work to be saved, we will do good works because we are saved. Humanly, we could never be good enough to earn salvation – no matter what we do. Paul tells us: ". . . all have sinned and fall short of the glory of God, . . ." (Romans 3:23). But, through Jesus Christ, we are given love unconditionally. Just as we will always love our children no matter what – He will always love us no matter what. When our children make a mistake now and then, we stand by them and still love them. In that same way, when we make mistakes or fall into temptation, God is quick to forgive us of our sins when we ask.

As parents, we have the responsibility of providing for our children's needs. And God, as our Heavenly Father, gives us what we need. Jesus, himself, says:

~ *Living in Blessings* ~

> *Which of you, if his son asks for bread, will give him a stone? . . . If you, then, though you are evil, know how to give good gifts to your children, how much more will your Father in heaven give good gifts to those who ask him! (Matthew 7:9, 11)*

Yes, God wants to give us blessings!

Blessing On Top of Blessing

In Proverbs, we learn:

> *...the Lord gives wisdom, and from his mouth come knowledge and understanding. He holds victory in store for the upright, he is a shield to those whose walk is blameless, for he guards the course of the just and protects the way of his faithful ones. (Proverbs 2:6-8)*

Do you see in this verse how the blessing is given for the fulfillment of the requirement? Victory is won for the upright, for those who practice integrity. He protects and defends those who follow His way of life. He watches over the events that take place in the life of those who are morally good. He protects the coming and going of those who are faithful to Him. Yes! God loves to pour down blessings on His children.

Because we love Him, God Himself tells us:

> *Because he loves me, says the Lord, I will rescue him; I will protect him, for he acknowledges my name. He will call upon me, and I will answer him; I will be with him in trouble, I will deliver him and honor him. With long life will I satisfy him and show him my salvation. (Psalm 91:14-16)*

~ CHAPTER THIRTEEN ~

Loving Him brings help. Acknowledging His name, His power and authority, brings protection. Praying brings answers, deliverance, and honor. These verses assure us that all His promises and blessings belong to those who love Him.

Refuge From the Storm

When we love the Lord, we receive so much more than we could ever give. Better still, we don't have to worry, draining our energies by focusing on all life's problems. Instead, we make the Lord the focus of our life. In turn, He becomes our rest and our refuge from life's storms. The writer of this Psalm tells us:

> *He who dwells in the shelter of the Most High will rest in the shadow of the Almighty. I will say of the Lord, 'He is my refuge and my fortress, my God, in whom I trust.' (Psalm 91:1-2)*

The following passages from Psalm 37 illustrate exactly how interactive our relationship with the Lord truly is and the simplicity of the process:

> *Trust in the Lord and do good; dwell in the land and enjoy safe pasture. (Verse 3)*

> *Delight yourself in the Lord and he will give you the desires of your heart. (Verse 4).*

> *Commit your way to the Lord; trust in him and he will do this: He will make your righteousness shine like the dawn, the justice of your cause like the noonday sun. (Verses 5, 6)*

...the power of the wicked will be broken, but the Lord upholds the righteous. (Verse 17)

The days of the blameless are known to the Lord, and their inheritance will endure forever. (Verse 18)

For the Lord loves the just and will not forsake his faithful ones. (Verse 28)

...there is a future for the man of peace.... the future of the wicked will be cut off. (Verses 37, 38).

The salvation of the righteous comes from the Lord; he is their stronghold in time of trouble. (Verse 39)

With God, you can defeat the giants in your life.

"Judge Not Lest You Be Judged"

As Christians, followers of Christ, we are not to "judge" others unwisely. When you see a fellow believer with seemingly overwhelming problems, you can't automatically assume that the problems or troubles have come upon that person because of a lack of faith or unbelief or as a punishment. Solomon reminds us that "time and chance happen to [us] all" (Ecclesiastes 9:11, Comments in brackets added). Jesus tells us:

~ CHAPTER THIRTEEN ~

> *Do not judge, or you too will be judged. For in the same way you judge others, you will be judged, and with the measure you use, it will be measured to you. (Matthew 7:1-2)*

His brother, James, also cautions us:

> *...Anyone who speaks against his brother or judges him speaks against the law and judges it... There is only one Lawgiver and Judge, the one who is able to save and destroy. But you – who are you to judge your neighbor? (James 4:11)*

Sometimes God allows us to go through things as He did Job for many different reasons. Sometimes He wants us to prove our faithfulness. James tells us:

> *...the testing of your faith develops perseverance. Perseverance must finish its work so that you may be mature and complete, not lacking anything. (James 1:3-4)*

Sometimes, it is to teach us a particular lesson. Sometimes, it is to purify us or to give us the ability to have compassion for others in similar situations. Whatever the reason, these types of situations will make us better people when we allow God to work in our lives. No matter what – through "thick and thin" – believe God's Word and have faith in knowing He is in control of your situations.

Keep in mind, this life wasn't meant to be problem-free, not even for those of us who love and serve the living God. Even Jesus Christ suffered. The writer of Hebrews tells us of Jesus: "... he learned obedience from what he suffered..." (Hebrews 5:8). And again, He suffered first, as our example:

~ Living in Blessings ~

> ...But if you suffer for doing good and you endure it, this is commendable before God. To this you were called, because Christ suffered for you, leaving you an example, that you should follow in his steps. (1 Peter 2:20-21)

Christ became the prime example of suffering wrong, for doing only those things that were right and good. Let His example be an encouragement to you:

> Consider him who endured such opposition from sinful men, so that you will not grow weary and lose heart. (Hebrews 12:3)

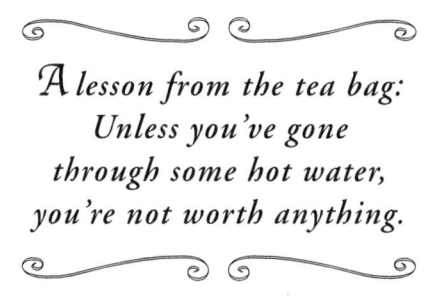

*A lesson from the tea bag:
Unless you've gone
through some hot water,
you're not worth anything.*

Suffering for Christ

Peter tells us we have a living hope of an inheritance which will never perish that is kept in Heaven for us. He says, too, that:

> In this you greatly rejoice, though now for a little while you may have had to suffer grief in all kinds of trials. These have come so that your faith ... may be proved genuine and may result in praise, glory and honor when Jesus Christ is revealed. (1 Peter 1:6-7)

~ CHAPTER THIRTEEN ~

Peter goes on to say:

> ...*do not be surprised at the painful trial you are suffering, as though something strange were happening to you.... If you are insulted because of the name of Christ, you are blessed, for the Spirit of glory and of God rests on you... if you suffer as a Christian, do not be ashamed, but praise God that you bear that name. (1 Peter 4:12, 14, 16)*

He wraps it up by saying:

> *So then, those who suffer according to God's will should commit themselves to their faithful Creator and continue to do good. (1 Peter 4:19)*

Sometimes if you've been going through some hard times, you may just feel like giving up and "throwing in the towel." You may wonder if it is really all worth it. Let me stress, "Yes, it is worth it!" Nothing we go through now can be compared to our reward in Heaven. Satan tries to enter our minds with his suggestions of weariness and defeat. Don't listen to him because God has the victory waiting for you. God even knew our enemy would try to take advantage of us in this way and inspired Paul to write:

> *Let us not become weary in doing good, for at the proper time we will reap a harvest if we do not give up. (Galatians 6:10)*

When you are trying to resolve a situation or problem, determine what you know is right to do in that situation and then give it over to God. Realize and confess that He is in control of all things. God allows us to be in a lot of situations where we can exercise our faith and trust in Him. As a word of encouragement, when things get really tough – it means there is a breakthrough and victory just around the corner.

Waiting on the Lord

We must realize God's schedule doesn't always coincide with the schedule we have planned. Most of the time, we want to see immediate results. But, God does things in His own timing because He can see the whole picture.

Our focus tends to be a very narrow one sometimes and can even change from day to day – moment to moment – according to our circumstances. But, God doesn't make decisions based on circumstances. During those times, when it seems God has been silent, remember, if we can "Be still before the Lord and wait patiently for him. . ." (Psalm 37:7), He will answer our prayers.

Differences in God's time table and ours applies not only to deliverance from situations we find ourselves in, but also to the purpose He has for our individual lives as well. God places desires in our hearts that lead us into our purpose. With those desires comes a season of preparation. Sometimes, we *think* we are ready, but only God *knows* when we are truly ready.

During this time of preparation, allow God to work in your life. Continue to be patient while the Holy Spirit refines you. Once you are in the place God wants you to be, He will give you the "green light" to forge ahead. God's timing is very important. Don't try to forge ahead of God or promote yourself – let God promote you.

If you move independently from Him, you'll be doing all the work. Instead, let God work through you. When you are in God's timing, then you will have the anointing of the Holy Spirit. It is the anointing that gives you the authority and the power to accomplish what He has given you to do. The anointing is what makes the difference.

~ CHAPTER THIRTEEN ~

You Are a New Person in Christ!

We know our sins have been forgiven through the death of Christ. We know that salvation is a gift from God – that it isn't earned. We know keeping the law will never grant us salvation or favor with Him. God has poured out His grace and mercy on us. And, because of His grace, we have been offered salvation and His favor.

Realizing this, should we continue in our sins or bad habits? Paul tells us: "By no means! We died to sin; how can we live in it any longer?" (Romans 6:2). He reminds us: "You, however, are controlled not by the sinful nature but by the Spirit, if the Spirit of God lives in you" (Romans 8:9). In Galatians, he also tells us: ". . . live by the Spirit, and you will not gratify the desires of the sinful nature" (Galatians 5:16). He goes on to say:

> *. . .if you live according to the sinful nature, you will die; but if by the Spirit you put to death the misdeeds of the body, you will live, because those who are led by the Spirit of God are sons of God. (Romans 8:13-14)*

As a believer, a follower of Jesus Christ, you are called God's child. Just as you pick up characteristics from your earthly parents, you should also find you are picking up more and more of the characteristics of your Heavenly Father. Peter tells us:

> *"But just as he who called you is holy, so be holy in all you do; for it is written: 'Be holy, because I am holy.' " (1 Peter 1:15-16)*

Through Christ, all things have been made new. You have a whole new way of life ahead of you. You no longer need to be controlled by those old things. But, you say: "I've tried to give it up and I can't – my old nature is too much a part of me." If you have accepted Christ as your Savior and the Holy Spirit is living in you, then you are in the process of overcoming that old nature. It no longer needs to control you, it is no longer your master. Remember that the Word of God tells us: ". . .if anyone is in Christ, he is a new creation; the old has gone, the new has come!" (2 Corinthians 5:17).

Becoming an "Overcomer"

The truth is, according to the Bible, you have choices. And, you can choose to change your ways that are contrary to God's ways. Maybe you can't make the changes, but the good news is God can. Agree with Paul when he said, "I can do everything through him [Christ] who gives me strength" (Philippians 4:13, Comments in brackets added). Yes, you do have strength through Christ. You may not be able to change all by yourself, but with the Lord's help, you can!

The indwelling Holy Spirit will help you to overcome if you really want to change. What was that comment thrown in there – "if you really want to change?" Have you said, "I don't want to give this up, even though I know it is wrong in God's eyes, I like doing this. Maybe God made a mistake to include it in His list of things that aren't good for us to do."

Sorry, that was a nice try, but our God doesn't make mistakes. Of course, some of these things may seem pleasurable for a season. Why else would we get caught up in some of those things that we know are harmful in the long run, to ourselves or to others? But, we can't take this lightly. The Word says: "Don't you know. . .you are slaves to the one whom you obey – whether you are slaves to sin, which leads to death, or to obedience, which leads to righteousness?" (Romans 6:16).

Don't think of it in terms of giving something up because you are actually just *replacing* sinful acts with righteous ones. You are coming out from under the control of that thing that has really been controlling you. You will find a burden lifted from you that you didn't even realize was there, and a sense of peace, freedom, and thanksgiving.

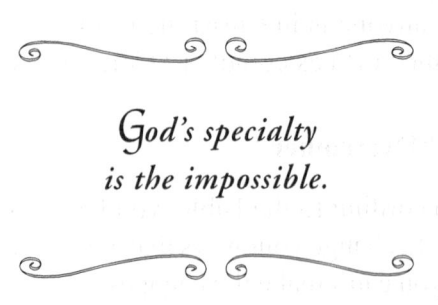

> *God's specialty is the impossible.*

Paul stresses that: ". . .by the Spirit you put to death the misdeeds of the body. . . (Romans 8:13). When Christ lives in you by the Holy Spirit, then you can and do have the victory over that sin or bad habit that has controlled you. Why? Because Christ has already overcome the world. John tells us:

> *. . . for everyone born of God overcomes the world. This is the victory that has overcome the world, even our faith. (1 John 5:4)*

Since by faith we accepted Christ, and as a result have been spiritually born of God, we are then given the Holy Spirit who helps us conquer these things that we no longer want controlling our lives.

Living God's Way

God expects us to live up to the conditions that He has set, so that we can receive all the blessings He has in store for us. Paul tells us:

Since we have these promises. . .let us purify ourselves from everything that contaminates body and spirit, perfecting holiness out of reverence for God. (2 Corinthians 7:1)

Paul continually stresses godly living:

For the grace of God. . .teaches us to say 'No' to ungodliness and worldly passions, and to live self-controlled, upright and godly lives in this present age, . . . (Titus 2:11-12)

Jesus has shown that He loves us more than anything by His ultimate sacrifice on the cross. The least we can do is show Him how much we love Him by walking in truth, applying His word, and lining our lives up with His own. If we believe Jesus is the foundation of our lives, then our lives will reflect that belief. Paul urges us:

. . .in view of God's mercy, to offer [our] bodies as living sacrifices, holy and pleasing to God – this is [our] spiritual act of worship" (Romans 12:1, Comments in brackets added)

Don't put it off any longer. Live in all the blessings and promises God has to offer you. All the examples that we have examined, showing us the conditions or requirements to be met in order to receive all He has for us, can be summed up in this statement by the Lord in Matthew:

But seek first his [God's] kingdom and his righteousness, and all these things will be given to you as well. (Matthew 6:33, Comments in brackets added)

~ CHAPTER THIRTEEN ~

When you seek God, you will find yourself already fulfilling these conditions. It is a little like playing tag – you have to know who is "it." The blessings aren't "it," so don't be pursuing and running after the blessings. God is "it," so be pursuing and running after Him. Then, in turn, He will pursue and run after you with all His blessings.

In all that you do, remember to praise and worship the God who offers you such an overwhelming treasure of love and blessings.

~ CHAPTER FOURTEEN ~

Receiving Healing and Prosperity

When you truly love someone, you want the best for them. That's the way it is with God. Because of His great love for all His children, the Lord wants to give us *all* good things – health, prosperity, well-being, and peace of mind. Jesus said: "I am come that they might have life, and that they might have it more abundantly" (John 10:10 KJV).

Yes, as His child, the omnipotent Creator of this universe cherishes *you* and has set His affections on you. That's right. The Lord wants to give you – His child – every good gift when you are faithful to Him. According to Psalm 149:4, God "delights" in you and in Psalm 37:4, we read: "Delight yourself in the Lord and He will give you the desires of your heart." When you are in the warmth of His Heavenly light, His blessings flow out and to and *through* you.

~ CHAPTER FOURTEEN ~

"By His Stripes We Are Healed"

By His willingness to die on the cross, Jesus Christ made spiritual healing and eternal life with God available to us. When Christ was willing to be beaten and physically abused before His crucifixion, He was allowing physical healing to be made available to us.

The great prophet Isaiah, 740 years before Christ was born, prophesied: ". . . by his wounds we are healed" (Isaiah 53:5). Christ's physical suffering paid the price for our healing. Peter echoes Isaiah's sentiments in the New Testament: ". . .by his wounds you have been healed" (1 Peter 2:24).

Interestingly, Isaiah spoke in the present tense and Peter in the past tense. Isaiah claimed salvation on faith long before Christ appeared on earth, and Peter claimed it with full knowledge and as an eyewitness to the saving grace of Jesus.

God Wants Us to Be in Good Health

God has said: ". . .I am the Lord, who heals you" (Exodus 15:26). Yes, the Lord is the one Who heals us. Even more, it is His will for us to be well and in good health. He didn't intend for us to be sick. The Psalmist tells us:

> *Praise the Lord, O my soul, and forget not all his benefits – who forgives all your sins and heals all your diseases, who redeems your life from the pit and crowns you with love and compassion, who satisfies your desires with good things so that your youth is renewed like the eagle's. (Psalm 103:2-5)*

In Matthew, we find an example of Jesus performing miracles of healing:

~ *Receiving Healing and Prosperity* ~

> *Jesus went through all the towns and villages, teaching. . .preaching. . .and healing every disease and sickness. (Matthew 9:35)*

Healing Power

The Bible records numerous occurrences of miraculous healings by Christ and for all kinds of people, from beggars, lepers and cripples to children and widows and community leaders – even an officer in the Roman army. As a matter of fact, John tells us that besides all the miracles that have been recorded, there were many others that were performed but weren't written down. Even though the disciples were witnesses to many more of these, it would have been almost impossible to record them all (See John 20:30, 21:25).

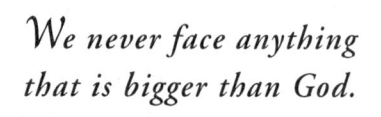

We never face anything that is bigger than God.

What were some of the kinds of sufferings that Jesus healed, and how did the majority of onlookers respond when they witnessed these miraculous events? Matthew tells us:

> *Great crowds came to him, bringing the lame, the blind, the crippled, the mute and many others, and laid them at his feet; and he healed them. The people were amazed when they saw the mute speaking, the crippled made well, the lame walking and the blind seeing. And they praised the God of Israel. (Matthew 15:30-31)*

At first, when the people saw these events taking place, they were surprised and filled with wonder. Then, they began to glorify and worship God.

~ CHAPTER FOURTEEN ~

In Luke, we find the twelve apostles also being given the power and authority by Jesus to heal and minister in miraculous ways:

> *When Jesus had called the Twelve together, he gave them power and authority to drive out all demons and to cure diseases, and he sent them out to preach the kingdom of God and to heal the sick. . .So they set out and went from village to village, preaching the gospel and healing people everywhere. (Luke 9:1-2, 6)*

It wasn't the disciples' own power that caused these healings. They were able to perform these miracles only through the power and authority that had been given to them by Jesus Christ. In Acts, we find an example of this power when Peter heals the crippled beggar:

> *Then Peter said. . . 'In the name of Jesus Christ of Nazareth, walk.' Taking him by the right hand, he helped him up, and instantly the man's feet and ankles became strong. He jumped to his feet and began to walk. (Acts 3:6-8)*

In these verses, Peter is using the authority that comes with using the "name" of Jesus Christ to bring healing to this man. Even today we use the "name" of others to give us authority we wouldn't otherwise have.

To illustrate this, let's look at a modern example in the business world. Say, for example, you work for Company A and your boss sends you to Company B to pick up some very important documents. If you just walked in off the street and asked for those documents, they wouldn't give them to you. But, if you go to Company B and tell them you represent Company A (using the "name" of the company) and show that you are authorized to pick up the documents, the papers would immediately be given to you.

~ Receiving Healing and Prosperity ~

Likewise, the men in these passages were using the authority of Jesus and didn't take any credit for the wonders and miracles that took place. They knew their source of power came from God. Peter tells the crowd:

> *'Men of Israel, why does this surprise you? Why do you stare at us as if by our own power or godliness we had made this man walk? The God of Abraham, Isaac and Jacob, the God of our fathers, has glorified his servant Jesus. . . . 'By faith in the name of Jesus, this man whom you see and know was made strong. It is Jesus' name and the faith that comes through him that has given this complete healing to him, as you can all see.' (Acts 3:12-13,16)*

After Jesus had been crucified and had risen, He appeared to His disciples. At this time, the power and authority to heal was given to all believers. Jesus said to them:

> *'And these signs will accompany those who believe: In my name. . .they will place their hands on sick people, and they will get well.' (Mark 16:17-18)*

Just like the early apostles and disciples, we have this same authority and power given to us today by Christ, if we are believers, to bring about miraculous healings in His name. When we use the "name" of Jesus, we are actually saying that we are His representatives and have His authority to back us. Further instruction is given by James:

> *Is any one of you sick? He should call the elders of the church to pray over him and anoint him with oil in the name of the Lord. And the prayer offered in faith will make the*

~ CHAPTER FOURTEEN ~

sick person well; the Lord will raise him up. (James 5:14-15)

In some instances, the faithful prayers of the elders in the church are sought to receive healing. The anointing with oil is used as a sign or symbol of the healing God will perform in response to their faith.

Different Methods of Healing

The evidence on healing that we see throughout both the Old and New Testaments is that the Lord used a variety of methods to bring healing to the people – sometimes through extraordinary, supernatural and miraculous circumstances and sometimes through down-to-earth, no-nonsense, and practical remedies.

God's healing is much like the physician's healing – sometimes He gives us immediate relief and sometimes we have to follow His instructions and take the proper "medication" to receive healing. After all, God is the "Great Physician."

One Biblical example of how God works through conventional means is found in the New Testament. Paul is advising Timothy to: "Stop drinking only water, and use a little wine because of your stomach and your frequent illnesses" (1 Timothy 5:23). Today, through research, we understand the health benefits of wine when used in moderation. Here, Paul was referring to wine's ability to help relieve stomach distress, aid in digestion, and combat certain bacteria.

Another example comes from the Book of Kings. The author tells us about the illness of Hezekiah and his close brush with death. The Lord heard the cries and prayers of Hezekiah and told him through the prophet Isaiah that He would heal him, as well as add fifteen years to his life. After Isaiah gave Hezekiah this message from the Lord, he said: ". . . 'Prepare a

~ Receiving Healing and Prosperity ~

poultice of figs'. They did so and applied it to the boil, and he recovered" (2 Kings 20:7). Figs were used for medicinal purposes in this ancient time and area. Scripture tells us the Lord healed Hezekiah, but we see from this example that divine healing doesn't always exclude the use of known remedies.

There are scriptures that tell us that Jesus "healed *all* the sick" and that He "went healing *every* disease and sickness." The evidence that is given to us throughout the New Testament shows us that even Jesus used a variety of methods to bring healing to the people. He brought healing with a word, a touch, by forgiving sin, by taking a hand, or through the faith of the one desiring healing. There are other instances in the Bible when Jesus healed people at the request of another. In response to the word of healing that Jesus spoke, those people also received healing, even though they weren't in His presence.

Let's take a look at the account of a man born blind and how he received his healing. Now, Jesus could have easily healed this blind man with a word or a touch, as He did the two blind men recorded in Matthew 9:27-29. Instead:

> . . .*he spit on the ground, made some mud with the saliva, and placed it on the man's eyes. 'Go,' he told him, 'wash in the Pool of Siloam' . . .So the man went and washed, and came home seeing. (John 9:6-7)*

In the instance of this blind man, applying a mixture to the wounded area plus obedience to His command to wash in a particular pool was needed for the healing to take place. What we have to keep in mind is that God heals each of us in the way that is best for us as individuals. Since we are each unique and one of a kind, he treats each of us as such – He treats us as individuals.

In this case, Jesus sent the blind man to his own special place to get his healing. Interestingly, this man could possibly have been healed immediately by Jesus' miraculous touch, but by Jesus putting the mud on his eyes, the man wouldn't truly "know" he was healed until he reached the pool and washed the mud away. The blind man by going to the pool showed His faith, belief, and acceptance of who Jesus Christ was, and, in effect, became "baptized" at the same time he was healed.

This story of the blind man is just one of many Biblical examples which shows us how Jesus knows our "hearts" like no one else can – how He knows us in the very depth of our being. Yes, Jesus Christ can get down deep into our inner soul where no one else can enter in, and understand our most secret needs and emotions. Through Jesus Christ both our spiritual and physical needs can be met, which in turn, will bring healing to both our minds and bodies.

You have to have a problem in order to have a miracle.

Forgiveness of Sin and Healing

Another interesting point that is revealed in this story about the blind man is that the disciples thought the man's blindness was caused by "sin" in either his life or in the lives of his parents. But, Jesus said, "Not so." The man was blind from birth for God's purposes:

> *'Neither this man nor his parents sinned,' said Jesus, 'but this happened so that the work of God might be displayed in his life. (John 9:3)*

Jesus plainly opposed the disciples' belief, as well as others of His day, who thought that *all* suffering came from sin in the sufferer's life or from the sin of their parents.

~ *Receiving Healing and Prosperity* ~

Now, there are times when sin could be the underlying factor in an illness. There are many habits and sins that people become involved in, even today, which can be damaging to their health, as well as to their children's health. What is the underlying sin in these instances – harming the body. It is because God loves us and made us and wants us to be healthy that He doesn't want us doing things to our bodies that will be harmful to them. Paul tells us:

> *Do you not know that your body is a temple of the Holy Spirit, who is in you, whom you have received from God? You are not your own; you were bought at a price. Therefore honor God with your body. (I Corinthians 6:19-20)*

Matthew gives us even more insight in this account of the paralytic who was healed by Jesus:

> *Some men brought to him a paralytic, lying on a mat. When Jesus saw their faith, he said to the paralytic, 'Take heart, son; your sins are forgiven.' (Matthew 9:2)*

Some of the teachers of the law had questions in their hearts, not understanding why Jesus was saying this. He replied:

> *Which is easier: to say, 'Your sins are forgiven,' or to say, 'Get up and walk'? . . . Then he said to the paralytic, 'Get up, take your mat and go home.' And the man got up and went home. (Matthew 9:5-7)*

James also refers to this possibility:

> *"And the prayer offered in faith will make the sick person well; the Lord will raise him up. If*

~ CHAPTER FOURTEEN ~

he has sinned, he will be forgiven. Therefore confess your sins to each other and pray for each other so that you may be healed." (James 5:15-16)

Here again we see in the Scriptures that not all illness is rooted in sin. James uses the conditional "if", signifying sin may or may not be the cause of an illness. Keep in mind that illness and disease are a part of our weakened human condition and can be brought on by many different factors.

Yes, You Can Believe in Healing Miracles

I am so glad God is in the healing business, aren't you? And did you know that He is the healer, not only of our bodies, but also of our minds, our emotions and our relationships. The Psalmist proclaims: "He heals the broken hearted and binds up their wounds" (Psalm 147:3).

No matter how we are healed, the most important point to remember is that God is the source of all our healing. Healing of any kind is a benefit that comes from the love He has for us – sometimes the healing is miraculous, sometimes not. But, God still does perform the supernatural, miraculous healing of Biblical times, and it can happen to you today just as it did in those days. We are told in Hebrews: "Jesus Christ is the same yesterday and today and forever" (Hebrew 13:8). What He did before, He will do again. If He healed people in the past, you know for a certainty that He will heal people today. The Apostle John stresses the heart of God in this statement:

Dear friend, I pray that you may enjoy good health and that all may go well with you, even as your soul is getting along well. (3 John 1: 2)

~ Receiving Healing and Prosperity ~

We can be so thankful that it is God's will to heal us and for us to be healthy.

God Wants Us to Prosper

Isn't it wonderful to know that you have a Heavenly Father who cares about your health? But, did you realize that He also cares about your finances because that is also a part of your well-being

Do you think God wants you to be poor and to live in poverty? Do you think such a lifestyle glorifies God? Of course not! The Bible tells us that God wants us to prosper in every way. Jesus said: "I have come that they may have life, and have it to the full" (John 10:10). And, in Psalms, we learn that those who fear the Lord and follow after Him will be blessed with prosperity:

> *Blessed are all who fear the Lord, who walk in His ways. You will eat the fruit of your labor; blessings and prosperity will be yours. (Psalm 128:1-2)*

As a review, to "fear the Lord" means to have reverential awe for Him. We are to respect His authority, and we are to honor, trust, and obey Him. Right reverence and respect for God is the basis for all godly living. In Proverbs, the book of wisdom, we are told: "To fear the Lord is to hate evil" (Proverbs 8:13). To continue, Paul stresses that God will supply our needs:

> *And God is able to make all grace abound to you, so that in all things at all times, having all that you need, you will abound in every good work. (2 Corinthians 9:8)*

God wants us to prosper so that we will always have the ability to be generous, both monetarily and in good deeds

~ CHAPTER FOURTEEN ~

towards others. Paul goes on to say: "You will be made rich in every way so that you can be generous on every occasion. . ." (2 Corinthians 9:11). In other words, our "abundance" is not to be kept to ourselves, but it is given to us so that we can share it with others. As a result of our generosity, God will be thanked and praised. You can be assured that if you follow this simple Biblical principle, then you'll find there's always more than enough for you *and* for you to give to others.

Have you considered the fact that the God we serve is the greatest giver of all? Do you realize He has set the example of giving for us. He was so willing to want to "give" us everything that He literally sacrificed, "gave" His own son for us. God was the very first giver.

The person who follows His example, enjoying and willfully giving, will receive blessing upon blessing from God in return for a generous spirit:

> *Give, and it will be given to you. A good measure, pressed down, shaken together and running over, will be poured into your lap. For with the measure you use, it will be measured to you. (Luke 6:38)*

In Proverbs 11:25, it states: "A generous man will prosper;" Paul advises us not to give reluctantly or because we feel we have to. No, the Lord doesn't want us to give grudgingly, for "God loves a cheerful giver" (2 Corinthians 9:7). Why don't you give it a try? Implement God's principle in your life, and see what blessings the Lord has "in store" for you. And always remember: ". . . whoever sows generously will also reap generously" (2 Corinthian 9:6).

Yes, wealth and prosperity are blessings and rewards from God. In Proverbs, we learn that "The blessing of the Lord brings wealth" (Proverbs 10:22) and that "Humility

~ Receiving Healing and Prosperity ~

and the fear of the Lord bring wealth and honor and life" (Proverbs 22:4).

It is wonderful to know that God is aware of our personal needs *before* we even have need of them and will amply supply our needs when we trust and depend on Him! Jesus tells us:

> *. . .do not worry about your life, what you will eat or drink; or about your body, what you will wear. . . . your heavenly Father knows that you need them. But seek first his kingdom and his righteousness, and all these things will be given to you as well. (Matthew 6:25, 32-33)*

When you seek God first and are faithful to Him, He'll provide for your needs. He will take care of you. What a loving, caring Heavenly Father we have. John says it best:

> *How great is the love the Father has lavished on us, that we should be called children of God! And that is what we are! (1 John 3:1)*

God Wants to Take Care of You

The Bible tells us that without a doubt, God wants to heal us, He wants us to be in good health, and He wants us to prosper. He wants to take care of us. He wants to give us good things. In Ephesians, Paul stresses that God is able "to do immeasurably more than all we ask or imagine, according to his power that is at work within us" (Ephesians 3:20). Also, remember Jesus said: ". . . how much more will your Father in heaven give good gifts to those who ask Him!" (Matthew 7:11).

The Lord wants to give you so much more than just the natural, physical comforts in life. His Word tells us that

~ CHAPTER FOURTEEN ~

He offers us life, forgiveness, mercy, strength, grace, peace, victory, love, and the ability to overcome through the power and might of the indwelling Holy Spirit. Yes! It is "'Not by might nor by power, but by my Spirit,' says the LORD Almighty" (Zechariah 4:6). God is capable, ready, willing and able to do more than you could ever humanly imagine!

> *Put everything in God's hand,
> then God's hand
> will be in everything.*

~ CHAPTER FIFTEEN ~

Yes! God Loves Me!

Many of us have heard the once popular song with the words, "Looking for love in all the wrong places." Sometimes we look to people for the unconditional love that only God can give. And, then we wonder why we're always disappointed. But, God is not like people. He will never let you down. Always remember this: *Nobody in all the world will ever love you like God loves you.* Take His "Word" for it, He will love you for all time – even into eternity.

You Are a Child of God

Your value comes from being rooted in knowing you belong to God. Being a child of God should give you all the self-worth you will ever need. A famous evangelist once said, "God doesn't sponsor flops." That's so true. You are made in God's image, and you are His workmanship.

~ CHAPTER FIFTEEN ~

In the Word of God, the Lord says He loves you. Yes, He loves *all* His children. So anyone who tells you otherwise is not speaking the truth. And, any thought that makes you think, "God doesn't love me" is not the truth. Believe what God says about you! Fill yourself up with what God says. See yourself as God sees you.

> *Jesus is able to lift you up and make your life significant.*

The following verses from the Bible have been personalized just for you. Each verse attests to the fact that God truly does love you and that in His eyes, you are very special:

> I have been redeemed and my sins forgiven through God's Son. (See Colossians 1:14).

> I am God's child, through faith in Christ Jesus. (See Galatians 3:26)

> I am Christ's friend. (See John 15:15).

> I am chosen, holy and dearly loved. (See Colossians 3:12).

> God has anointed me and put His Spirit in my heart. (See 2 Corinthians 1:21-22).

> I have been given favor and honor. (See Psalm 84:11).

> I am blessed because I trust in the Lord. (See Psalm 84:12).

> In all things, I am more than a conqueror through Christ who loves me. (See Romans 8:37).

~ *Yes! God Loves Me!* ~

I am a member of Christ's body. (See 1 Corinthians 12:27).

I am the righteousness of God, through Christ. (See 2 Corinthians 5:21).

I walk in love. (See John 13:34).

I live by faith. (See Hebrews 10:38)

The power that raised Jesus from the dead, dwells in me. (See Ephesians 1:19-20)

Through Christ, I have direct access to the Father, by His Spirit. (See Ephesians 2:18)

My life will be exceedingly abundant, because His power is at work in me. (See Ephesians 3:20)

I can do everything with the help of Christ who gives me the strength. (See Philippians 4:13)

God has given me a spirit of power, of love and of a sound mind. (See 2 Timothy 1:7 KJV)

I am the salt and light of the earth. (See Matthew 5:12,14)

I have been chosen and appointed to bear fruit. (See John 15:16)

I am God's temple and His Spirit lives in me. (See 1 Corinthians 3:16)

No weapon formed against me will prevail. (Isaiah 54:17)

~ CHAPTER FIFTEEN ~

I have victory through Christ. (See 1 Corinthians 15:57)

NOTHING in all creation can separate me from the LOVE OF GOD! (See Romans 8:39)

Judge yourself by how God sees you – not as others may think of you or even as you might think of yourself. Believe what *God says* about you. Through Christ, you are not defeated – you are a conqueror. The triumphant, victorious Christ is living in you through the indwelling Holy Spirit. You are not a victim, but a victor. As Paul sums it up: ". . .we are God's workmanship. . ." (Ephesians 2:10).

> *Agree to be the person God wants you to be.*

Knowing Him

I've thought about how I've always known *of* God and have learned *about* Him. And, I have continued to learn more and more *about* Him through the years. But, I also see how He is continually teaching me to *know* Him on a more personal level, in a more intimate way.

To "know" Him means not just as Creator and Savior, but as a friend who remains close to my heart. He is always reaching out to me as I reach out to Him. Likewise, He will always be there for you, reaching out to you as you reach out to Him. Isn't it wonderful such a close relationship is possible!

Love Letters for the Soul

Think for a moment how you feel towards someone you love. You want to do what pleases them, right? We have previously seen that our faith in God, trusting Him and believing His word, brings Him pleasure. You may be thinking: "Yes, and I love God, but what else can I do to show Him how much I love Him and how thankful I am for all He has done for me?" Jesus answers that question for you:

> *'If you love me, you will obey what I command. . . .Whoever has my commands and obeys them, he is the one who loves me. . . 'If anyone loves me, he will obey my teaching. . .(John 14:15, 21, 23)*

Have you noticed the trend; what God has required of us, or what Jesus has asked of us, He has done first. God loved us first and showed us by sending His Son to us. Then Jesus in turn declared:

> *If you obey my commands, you will remain in my love, just as I have obeyed my Father's commands and remain in his love." (John 15:10)*

Jesus continued by calling us His friends:

> *You are my friends if you do what I command. . . .I have called you friends, for everything that I learned from my Father I have made known to you. (John 15:14-15)*

> *The Apostle John emphasizes how we can show our love to God: "This is love for God: to obey his commands" (I John 5:3). Again he tells us: "And this is love: that we walk in obedience to his commands. . ." (2 John 1:6)*

This indicates we need to read the Bible – His word – so that we know what His teachings and commandments are. We

~ CHAPTER FIFTEEN ~

don't want to depend on others to tell us. We want to find out for ourselves.

Some call the Gospels, His "love letters" to us. What do we do with love letters? We treasure them and cherish them, don't we? We relish every word, reading them over and over again until they are an indelible part of our memory. That is exactly what God wants you to do with His Word – treat the Scriptures like "love letters for your soul."

Obeying God's Commands

Sometimes, such words as "command" and "obey" frighten people or turn them off, but this shouldn't be. We should cherish the commands of God. Why? Because God's commandments teach us how to love like God loves. In a Psalm that David wrote, he said of God's law:

> *The law of the Lord is perfect, reviving the soul. The statues of the Lord are trustworthy, making wise the simple. The precepts of the Lord are right, giving joy to the heart. The commands of the Lord are radiant, giving light to the eyes. The fear of the Lord is pure, enduring forever. The ordinances of the Lord are sure and altogether righteous. They are more precious than gold, than much pure gold; they are sweeter than honey, than honey from the comb. By them is your servant warned; in keeping them there is great reward. (Psalm 19:7-11)*

The Israelite who wrote Psalm 119, said of God's law:

> *Blessed are they whose ways are blameless, who walk according to the law of the Lord. (Verse 1)*

I rejoice in following your statures as one rejoices in great riches. (Verse 14)

Your statutes are my delight; they are my counselors. (Verse 24)

The law from your mouth is more precious to me than thousands of pieces of silver and gold. (Verse 72)

Oh, how I love your law! I meditate on it all day long. (Verse 97)

Your statutes are my heritage forever; they are the joy of my heart. (Verse 111)

Your statutes are wonderful; therefore I obey them. (Verse 129)

Great peace have they who love your law, and nothing can make them stumble. (Verse 165)

God's law shows us His character – His righteousness, His love, and His righteous judgment. They bring us wisdom, insight, and understanding.

Actions Speak Louder Than Words

In Deuteronomy, Chapter Five, we find a list of the *Ten Commandments*. As you study them, you will see that the first four commandments tell us how we can show love towards God, and the remaining six tell us how we can show love towards others (technically speaking, most show what *not* to do). When Jesus was asked which was the greatest commandment in the Law, He replied:

~ CHAPTER FIFTEEN ~

Love the Lord your God with all your heart and with all your soul and with all your mind. This is the first and greatest commandment. And the second is like it: Love your neighbor as yourself. All the Law and the Prophets hang on these two commandments. (Matthew 22:37-40)

Jesus' first statement summed up the first four commandments and His second comment summed up the last six.

We can *say* we have love, but if we don't *show* it with our actions, it's not really love. If we possess the real thing, there will be evidence in the way we live our lives to prove it. John implores us to follow our words of love with action: "Dear children, let us not love with words or tongue, but with actions and in truth" (1 John 3:18).

Christ has once again set the standard for us:

'A new command I give you: Love one another. As I have loved you, so you must love one another. By this all men will know that you are my disciples, if you love one another.' (John 13:34-35)

The commandment itself was not new, but His disciples now had a new understanding of what it meant to love others. They experienced, first hand, Christ's love for them. Walking with Him they had the opportunity to watch Him on a daily basis, as He treated others with compassion, mercy, and righteous judgment.

Jesus again said: "My command is this: Love each other as I have loved you" (John 15:12). And, how did Jesus love us? Not just with words, but with the ultimate action: "Greater love has no one than this, that he lay down his life for his friends" (John 15:13). Yes, Christ was willing to go the whole way – even to the point of death to show His love for us.

When something is repeated, we know it must be important. Just a few verses later, Jesus again says: "This is my command: Love each other" (John 15:17).

The Apostle Paul tells us:

> . . .whatever other commandments there may be, are summed up in this one rule: 'Love your neighbor as yourself.' Love does no harm to its neighbor. Therefore love is the fulfillment of the law. (Romans 13:9-10)

The Apostle John instructs us to:

> . . .love one another, for love comes from God. . . .since God so loved us, we also ought to love one another. . .if we love one another, God lives in us and his love is made complete in us. . .And he has given us this command: Whoever loves God must also love his brother. (1 John 4:7,11,12,21).

Are you beginning to have some understanding, some insight into why we can now keep the law, where as, in the past it was impossible for us. Before we accepted Christ, the law was just a reminder of our sins and our need for a Savior. But, Jesus came as our Savior and fulfilled the law by drawing on the Father's love, and in the same way, we fulfill the law by drawing on His love through the Holy Spirit that we have been given:

> *And hope does not disappoint us, because God has poured out His love into our hearts by the Holy Spirit, whom He has given us. (Romans 5:5)*

~ CHAPTER FIFTEEN ~

True Love

True love shows itself in the way we think and react to our life and to others. It's a constructive, building, sharing, and helping way of life. This love originates from God, "for love comes from God," and reflects His character in each one us. In turn, as His children, we reflect His love and pass it on. Paul defined true love better than anyone ever has:

> *Let people meet Jesus when they meet you.*

> *Love is patient, love is kind. It does not envy, it does not boast, it is not proud. It is not rude, it is not self-seeking, it is not easily angered, it keeps no record of wrongs. Love does not delight in evil but rejoices with the truth. It always protects, always trusts, always hopes, always perseveres. (1 Corinthians 13:4-7)*

Trusting in the Lord

You can't trust someone you don't know. When you come to "know" God and realize the true dimensions of His love, you can easily trust Him and have faith in His every word. You won't find it difficult to understand how He wants the best things for you. It will become easy for you to realize that more than anything, your Heavenly Father wants to bless you and wants you to receive all His promises.

God's love created you. Christ's sacrificial love is what saves you. The Holy Spirit's love will guide you. You can be certain that no one knows you like God does, and no one will ever love you like He can.

As you continue down life's journey, you can "rest" in the confidence and knowledge that the Lord cares about *you*, cherishes *you*, and will never forsake *you*. Does God love you? A big, emphatic "yes!" And now, you *know* He does!

The Love of the Bride for the Bridegroom

In Revelation, Christ is referred to as the "Bridegroom" and we are called His "Bride." This future scene reveals to us the intimate relationship that spiritually exists between God and His people:

> *Let us rejoice and be glad and give him glory! For the wedding of the Lamb [Christ, see John 1:29] has come, and his bride [His people] has made herself ready. (Revelation 19:7, Comments in brackets added)*

As the "Bride," shouldn't Christ be the first thing you think about in the morning and the last thing you think about at night, as well as every moment in between? Think about the first time you were in love. You couldn't stop thinking about your "true love," could you? That's the way you should be about Jesus. You should be "passionate" about Him. After all, He was "passionate" enough to die for you!

And, God wants to spend time with you, the same way you would want to spend time with the love of your life. As you spend private time with Him, you will discover it will change your life – for an eternity. So, let His love be with you every hour, every day, and in every circumstance.

From a Loving God to You

As you continue on life's journey and in your Christian walk, I invite you to read the promises from the passage in Deuteronomy, Chapter 28, verses 1 through 13. The blessings in this section have especially been an inspiration to me in my walk with the Lord. It is filled with words of

~ CHAPTER FIFTEEN ~

encouragement and reassurance of the divine love of God. In these verses are His promises for your life. Moses told the Israelites: "All these blessings will come upon you and accompany you if you obey the Lord your God" (Deuteronomy 28:2).

For your convenience, I have paraphrased these blessings and set them out so you can refer to them often. You will come to experience in your own life that the Lord is "the same yesterday, today and forever." So are His Words. The words spoken by Moses relay from God the blessings He wants to bestow on His people. They apply just as much to us in our present day as they did to the people who lived when Moses first spoke them:

> I will be blessed wherever I go, whether to the city or to the country.
>
> My children will be blessed and the work that I do will be blessed.
>
> I will be blessed with plenty of food.
>
> I will be blessed when I come in and blessed when I go out.
>
> The enemies who rise up against me will be defeated before me.
>
> The Lord will send a blessing on everything that I set my hand to do.
>
> The Lord my God will bless me where I live.
>
> I will be holy to God because I keep His commands and walk in His ways.

~ Yes! God Loves Me! ~

Others will see how God has blessed me because I belong to Him.

The Lord will grant me abundant prosperity – in my children, in my livelihood – in the place He has given me to live.

He will bless all the work of my hands.

I will lend to many, but I won't need to borrow.

The Lord will make me the head and not the tail.

I will always be at the top, never at the bottom, because I carefully follow the ways of the Lord and worship only Him.

[Paraphrased from Deuteronomy. 28:2-13]

Dear Friend, I certainly hope this book has been a blessing to you, and I pray that it will touch your heart in just the right way to meet your personal needs. God, your Creator, knows your wants, your desires and how to fill the lack that is in your life – even before you ever ask. You can be sure He will provide abundantly for your every need. Why? Because He loves *you!*

No one is like you, O Lord. You are great. Your name is mighty in power. You are the true God, the living God, the eternal King. You are my God. (Jeremiah 10:6, 10)

Now, we give you thanks and praise your glorious name. (I Chronicles 29:13)

About the Author

Nancy L. Anderson was born and raised in Pennsylvania. She currently resides in Florida with her husband, Carl. She is a graduate of both the *National Education Center* and *The Protocol School of Washington* (DC). Nancy attended *ORU Ministry Training and Development Institute* and is a member of the *American Christian Writers Association*. She has been active in both local and international women's ministries

Nancy's "heart's desire" is to see healing – physically, emotionally, and spiritually – manifested in the body of Christ. Her prayer is taken from Ephesians 3:17 – that all may be rooted and established in love, having the power, to understand how wide and long and high and deep is the love of Christ.

ORDER INFORMATION

To order copies of this book, please visit our website at:

www.e-eaglesrest.com

or send $12.95 + $2 shipping & handling for each book to:

Eagles Rest
PO Box 470544
Celebration, Florida 34747-0544

* Florida residents please add 6% sales tax *

Also Available at Your Christian Bookstore!

To contact the author, please write to Nancy Anderson care of the address above or e-mail:
nlandrsn@aol.com

──── ORDER NOW ────

ORDER INFORMATION

**To order copies of this book,
please visit our website at:**

www.e-eaglesrest.com

or send $12.95 + $2 shipping & handling
for each book to:

Eagles Rest
PO Box 470544
Celebration, Florida 34747-0544

* Florida residents please add 6% sales tax *

Also Available at Your Christian Bookstore!

To contact the author, please write to
Nancy Anderson care of the address above or e-mail:
nlandrsn@aol.com

———— **ORDER NOW** ————